A charged silence fell between them.

Sammy was intensely aware of the closeness of her body, the soft floral scent that was always a part of Beth. With just the two of them alone inside the cozy cabin, it seemed they were isolated from the rest of the world.

He stepped backward, breaking the spell. Protecting Beth was his job, and he'd better remember that fact. "I'll get the rest of the stuff in before it gets too dark."

"Right," she quickly agreed, her cheeks flushed pink. "Lots to do before I get settled in."

"Before we get settled in," he corrected.

"I already told you—I'm fine out here. Perfectly safe. No need—"

"I'm staying," he insisted. "At least for tonight."

APPALACHIAN PERIL

USA TODAY Bestselling Author

DEBBIE HERBERT

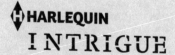

As always, to my husband, Tim; my sons, Byron and Jacob; and my father, J.W. Gainey. Much love to you all!

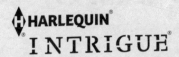

ISBN-13: 978-1-335-13596-4

Appalachian Peril

Copyright © 2020 by Debbie Herbert

This edition published by arrangement with Harlequin Books S.A.

For questions and comments about the quality of this book, please contact us at CustomerService@Harlequin.com.

Harlequin Enterprises ULC
22 Adelaide St. West, 40th Floor
Toronto, Ontario M5H 4E3, Canada
www.Harlequin.com

Printed in U.S.A.

Recycling programs for this product may not exist in your area.

USA TODAY bestselling author **Debbie Herbert** writes paranormal romance novels reflecting her belief that love, like magic, casts its own spell of enchantment. She's always been fascinated by magic, romance and gothic stories. Married and living in Alabama, she roots for the Crimson Tide football team. Her eldest son, like many of her characters, has autism. Her youngest son is in the US Army. A past Maggie Award finalist in both young adult and paranormal romance, she's a member of the Georgia Romance Writers of America.

Books by Debbie Herbert

Harlequin Intrigue

Appalachian Prey
Appalachian Abduction
Unmasking the Shadow Man
Murder in the Shallows
Appalachian Peril

Harlequin Nocturne

Bayou Magic

Bayou Shadow Hunter
Bayou Shadow Protector
Bayou Wolf

Dark Seas

Siren's Secret
Siren's Treasure
Siren's Call

Visit the Author Profile page at Harlequin.com.

CAST OF CHARACTERS

Beth Wynngate—The estrangement from her late father weighs heavily upon artistic and sensitive Beth. When she begins to receive increasingly threatening correspondence and is being stalked, Beth flees back to Appalachia and inadvertently falls into the arms of the man she blames for the estrangement from her family.

Sammy Armstrong—As a sheriff's deputy in a small mountain town, Sammy has fallen into a predictable routine with people he grew up with—until the night he's summoned to the Wynngate estate and encounters Beth after their disastrous past meeting.

Aiden Wynngate—Adopted by Judge Wynngate, Aiden has followed in his stepfather's footsteps to pursue a career as an attorney with ambitions to rise to a judgeship.

Dorsey Lambert—He served a long prison term on a federal conviction, thanks to a harsh sentence from Judge Wynngate. Dorsey is determined to seek his own brand of Southern justice upon his release.

Judge Wynngate—A proud patriarch with a rigid moral code. He was well respected in the courtroom and in his community. But did his outward polish belie dark secrets?

Chapter One

He'd found her. Again.

The chill churning Beth's insides had nothing to do with the biting Appalachian wind and everything to do with the letter in her hand. She wanted to fling it into the snow, let the white paper blend and melt into the icy flakes coating the mansion's lawn. But curiosity and a sense of self-preservation would not allow her to act so foolish. She looked up from the stack of mail in her hand and scanned the area.

Nothing marred the pristine white landscape of the exclusive Falling Rock community. Stately homes banked the lanes of the gated subdivision, and smoke curled from the chimneys of several houses. On the surface, all was cozy, civilized and well contained.

Was he watching her now? Delighting in her fear? Beth inhaled the frigid air and braced her shoulders. She wouldn't give him the satisfaction. This was a dangerous game the recently released convict played. If he'd meant physical harm, he'd already had the opportunity to do so in Boston when he broke into her condo.

She closed the mailbox lid and strolled up the driveway, even curled her lips in the semblance of a smile—just in case he was watching from the safety of the woods that lined the mountain's ridge. *Take that, Lambert.* At last she reached the front door, and her numb fingers fumbled at the doorknob for a moment before she pushed her way inside.

The warmth enveloped Beth as she locked the door behind her and leaned against it, her knees suddenly no more substantial than pudding. The pile of letters slipped from her fingers and dropped to the marble floor.

Movement flickered at the end of the long hallway. Cynthia passed by, wearing black pants and an eggplant-colored cashmere sweater that was a perfect foil for her brown hair highlighted with caramel streaks. How could anyone look so good so soon after waking? Beth sighed as she removed a striped knitted hat, her hair still wet from an early-morning shower. She hung up her coat on the antique hall tree, kicked off her shoes and picked up the fallen mail, placing her letter at the back. No need to worry Cynthia about that. This was her problem.

"Morning," Beth called as she entered the den and sank onto the leather sofa across from the fireplace. Abbie had already lit a fire, and the oak logs crackled and hissed, releasing a smoky, woodsy aroma.

"Morning. Would you like Abbie to bring you a cup of coffee?" Cynthia asked. "She's in the kitchen making it now."

Beth resisted a rueful smile. Cynthia fell naturally into the hostess role, but in fact, this house belonged to *Beth* now, not her stepmother. What was Cynthia even doing there? Usually she preferred to stay in Atlanta, close to her son. Beth picked up the mug on the end table beside her. "No coffee. I already have green tea."

"So healthy you are." Cynthia shot her an indulgent smile. "You and your herbal teas. Is that what's popular in Boston with the young crowd? As for me, I need a strong dose of caffeine."

Beth tucked her stockinged feet beneath her and sipped the tea, wishing it were a Bloody Mary. Anything to take the edge off the unease rippling down her spine. Was Lambert out there now? How much longer would he hound her? Hadn't she suffered enough for, according to the convict, the so-called sins of her father?

"Beth? Beth!" Cynthia leaned in front of her,

waving a hand in front of her face. "What's wrong with you?"

"N-nothing," she lied.

Cynthia's smooth forehead creased, and she straightened. "I was talking to you, and you stared out the window looking, well, frightened."

Cynthia might be on the self-absorbed side, but she was observant. Too observant. Beth wiggled her toes, considering how much to divulge.

Cynthia eased into a nearby chair. "Go on. Tell me. I'll help if I can."

She'd always been that way. A buffer between Beth and her stern father. Judge Wynngate had remained aloof and unapproachable to his only child right up until his death seven months ago. The chance for a proper father-daughter reconciliation was over.

"I had a bit of trouble in Boston," she admitted. "Somebody had been following me, even broke into my condo once."

"That's terrible." Cynthia drew back, placing a bejeweled hand with well-manicured nails against her chest. "Did the police catch the intruder?"

Beth shook her head, inwardly wincing as she recalled the cop's skepticism when she'd told him about the strange intrusion. "I'm not even sure they believed me when I reported the break-in."

"That doesn't make sense. Why wouldn't they?"

"Because nothing was stolen. My stuff had been rearranged, though. My journal and papers were taken from my bedroom and laid open on the kitchen table."

Cynthia gasped. "Why, that's—"

"Here's your coffee. One cream, no sugar."

Abbie placed the steaming mug on the table and gazed at Beth, her freckled face paler than normal and her brown eyes wide with concern. So she'd overheard.

"Thank you, Abigail."

At Cynthia's dismissive tone, Abbie hurried from the room, avoiding meeting Beth's eyes, which were filled with a silent apology for her stepmother's terse manner. Cynthia affixed her sharp gaze on Beth. "Go on."

Beth realized she wanted—no, *needed*—to talk to someone about her fear. Someone who'd take her seriously. And didn't her stepmother deserve to know about the continued slander Lambert had flung against her dad, Cynthia's late husband? She drew a deep breath and plunged ahead.

"The thing is, just a couple days before that happened, I'd received a threatening letter that said I have to pay for my father's corruption."

"Corruption?" Cynthia's lipsticked mouth fell open. "What's that supposed to mean? Edward was aboveboard in every way."

"I don't know. That's all the note said. I immediately suspected it was written by Dorsey Lambert."

Cynthia's face scrunched in displeasure. "I'd hoped to never hear that name again."

They fell silent, remembering the troublesome case of the drug dealer who'd been led from Judge Wynngate's courtroom, defiant and screaming about corruption in the justice system. Specifically, against the honored judge himself. Lambert had vowed revenge and her father had taken the matter so seriously that he'd installed an elaborate security system for their Atlanta estate. Too bad he hadn't done the same for this house in the North Georgia mountains.

"At least the Boston police checked out that lead for me," she said at last. "Turns out Dorsey Lambert was released from prison only two weeks ago."

"Did they question him?"

"Not personally. They contacted Atlanta PD, who went to the address Lambert provided the Georgia Department of Corrections. His mother vouched for him. Said he was living with her, working a steady job and completely off drugs."

"Of course she did," Cynthia said with an elegant lift of her chin. "What mother wouldn't provide an alibi for her child?"

"Exactly." Beth stared at her stepmother, wondering if Cynthia remembered doing much the same for her son, Aiden. Cynthia's protection of Aiden had come at Beth's expense, and her father had sided with his wife. The entire incident had created a distance from her dad that was never bridged before his death.

Old news. Let it go. Beth drew a deep breath. "Anyway, after getting that note I returned to the Boston PD to report the latest incident, and they kind of gave me the brush-off. Had me fill out a report and said they'd look into the matter." Beth stopped, flushing as she remembered how the cop on duty had lifted his eyebrows as she'd relayed what happened. He clearly thought she'd been spooked by an admittedly creepy letter and was making mountains of molehills.

"You should have told me earlier. I can make a few phone calls and have the Boston police prodded to do a thorough investigation."

Beth had considered it, of course. But winter break from her art teaching job had been around the corner, and she'd hoped it would all blow over by the time she returned. Her fingers tapped the pile of mail. Clearly, matters had not blown over with Lambert.

Cynthia's gaze dropped to the mail. "What's the matter? Did you get another letter?"

Sighing, Beth picked it up and stared at the envelope, which was postmarked Atlanta and had no return mailing information. Her name and address were printed in a standard computer font. She turned it over and picked at the edge.

"Shouldn't you be wearing gloves?"

"Too late now." Beth ripped it open, then frowned at the tiny scraps of paper littering the bottom.

"What is it?" Cynthia asked, leaning forward.

"I'm not sure." She emptied the bits of paper on the coffee table and spread them out. The small pieces had crisp edges, as though they'd been precisely cut with scissors or some other sharp tool. They were black and white and gray with printed text on the back, obviously clipped from a newspaper. She tried to arrange the text in some logical order but failed. Next, she arranged the scraps on the reverse side and gazed down at the jagged newspaper photo that emerged. Fear fizzed the nape of her neck.

She recognized the photograph. It had been shot at one of the few charitable events she'd attended with her father three years earlier. The judge was seated at a head table, Cynthia and her son, Aiden, on his right, and Beth at his immediate left. Her father held a wineglass in the air, proposing a toast to the guests and thanking them for their attendance.

In the midst of the varying shades of pixilated gray, a red marker circled Beth's body, and in the center of her chest was a red dot.

A lethal target mark.

"Oh my God," Cynthia said. With a loud thud, she set her coffee mug on the table. "I'll call Sheriff Sampson to come here at once. I really wished you had put on gloves like I asked."

"Me, too," she murmured, eyes fixed on the angry red dot.

An unexpected, warm pressure landed on her right shoulder, and Beth jumped to her feet. Twisting around, she half expected to find Lambert had sneaked in and was upon them. Instead, she faced Abbie's troubled eyes.

"Who would do something like this?" Abbie breathed, pressing her hands to her cheeks.

"I can only think of one person."

"Call the sheriff's office," Cynthia said crisply into her cell phone. It instantly obeyed her voice command, and the digital ring buzzed through the den.

"We could just go down to the station," Beth

pointed out. If the local officers were anything like the Boston PD, they wouldn't find this latest letter an emergency worthy of their immediate attention.

Cynthia waved an impatient hand, phone pressed to an ear. "I'd like to speak to Harlan Sampson," she demanded.

She and Abbie exchanged a look. How like her stepmother to go straight to the top of the chain. "This is Mrs. Cynthia Wynngate of Falling Rock. It's a matter of the utmost importance."

It was a familiar tone that both embarrassed and irritated Beth. Still, she had to admit that Cynthia's air of confident privilege was one that certainly got results.

"What do you mean he's not in? I need to speak with him at once." Her lips pursed. "A conference, you say? When will he be back?" Pause. "Then send out your next highest-ranking officer. I'll explain when he gets here. The address is 2331 Apple Orchard Lane."

Cynthia tapped a button, then dropped the phone on the sofa. "We should expect them in the next fifteen minutes or so. Abbie, make more coffee and heat up those cheese Danish rolls in the refrigerator."

Abbie slowly returned to the kitchen, casting troubled glances over her shoulder.

Cynthia retrieved her phone, aimed it at the macabre cut-up puzzle and snapped a photo. "The officer will collect this for evidence. Figured it wouldn't hurt for us to keep a backup photo. You can't be too careful. Do you have a copy of the first letter?"

"The Boston PD kept it."

She gave a quick nod, already in her familiar take-charge mode. "We'll have Harlan contact them and coordinate an investigation."

"You really think they'll do anything?" Beth asked doubtfully.

"Of course. I contributed to Harlan's reelection campaign. If nothing else, he'll investigate as a favor to me."

A new worry nagged at Beth. What if they sent Officer Armstrong over to the house? No, no. Surely not. Cynthia had asked for the next in line to the sheriff. Hopefully, that person wasn't Armstrong. Could she really be that unlucky? Hadn't her morning been bad enough?

She stared out the patio door with its panoramic view of the Appalachian Mountains. Snow brushed the tips and limbs of the trees and cleanly blanketed the ground.

Except for the large footprints originating at the edge of the woods and ending at their back porch.

Chapter Two

Sammy sighed as he finished his grits, slapped the cash on the counter and took a final gulp of iced tea. Yeah, he was a cop, so he should have been drinking the proverbial coffee and eating doughnuts. Call him a rebel.

"Trouble?" Jack asked, collecting the money and stuffing it in the till.

"Nah. Just duty calling. Catch you later."

He strolled to the cruiser, refusing to acknowledge the slight ping he'd experienced when the dispatcher had given him the name and address. No big deal, he told himself as he drove the short distance from Lavender to Blood Mountain. No need to think Mrs. Wynngate's stepdaughter would be visiting. No reason to believe there was danger brewing.

He waved to the security guard at the gate and breezed into the Falling Rock community with its rows of manicured homes. Blood Mountain was only half the size of its neighbor and sparsely inhabited except for this one exclusive subdivision. When people like Cynthia Wynngate called, they expected immediate attention, no matter the problem. He'd heard that Mrs. Wynngate's husband had died many) months ago. At least he wouldn't be stepping into a domestic disturbance situation. Those were the worst.

He knew exactly which showcase house belonged to the Wynngates, even if he hadn't been there in years. Sammy parked in the semicircular brick driveway and strode to the door, automatically surveying the area and cataloging details.

The Massachusetts license plate on the sleek BMW was the first sign of trouble.

Cynthia Wynngate's cold welcome at the door— "What took you so long to get here?"— was the second sign.

The final confirmation of trouble was the woman pacing the den. Pewter eyes, cool as gunmetal, slammed into him—she was clearly as unhappy to see him as he was to cross paths with her again. A younger girl he didn't recognize stood in the corner of the room, polishing a cherry hutch, trying to act inconspicuous but watching everything from the corner of her eyes.

Mrs. Wynngate didn't bother with introductions. He'd met her a few times over the years at local charity events and political fund-raisers. Not that she'd remember him. He was a law enforcement officer, a guy with a badge who served a function if she ever needed his service. Nothing more. She waved a hand at the coffee table as she sank onto a sofa. "Beth, tell him what's going on."

Beth uncrossed her arms and reluctantly made her way over, pointing at scraps of paper littering the table. "This came in the mail today."

He took a seat and peered down. "What is this? A cut-up old newspaper photo?"

Beth leaned over him, and he inhaled the clean scent of shampoo and talcum powder. A sudden, inexplicable urge to pull her into his lap and inhale her sweet freshness nearly overwhelmed him. *Stop it. Concentrate on the job.*

"Yes," she answered. "The photo's from many years ago. And that red dot is where he marked my chest."

The crimson ink made the hairs on his forearms rise. Why would anyone want to harm Beth? Perhaps it had been a particularly bad breakup with a boyfriend. Or an encounter with a guy who'd harbored hidden stalker behavior. "Any idea who might have sent this?"

"Dorsey Lambert," Beth answered at once.

"He threatened retaliation against Dad when he was sentenced twelve years back."

His forehead creased. The name didn't ring a bell. "But that was a long time ago. How can you be so sure—"

"They released him two weeks ago. Within days, I got a letter in Boston saying I'd have to pay for my father's corruption."

Mrs. Wynngate made a ticking noise of disgust as she rose from her seat and signaled to the young girl by the hutch. "Such a ridiculous accusation. Abbie, see if the officer would like coffee or refreshments."

Sammy flashed a quick smile in the girl's direction and held up a hand. "No, thanks," he told her, returning his attention to the photograph.

A disgruntled ex-con. Should be easy enough to track down the guy and have him questioned. He was obviously trying to scare Beth, but odds were he'd never take action. Often, these kinds of cowardly threats amounted to nothing more than bluster. But he'd definitely investigate. If this Lambert guy was released on parole rather than end-of-sentence, then he'd report the threats to Lambert's parole officer and have his parole revoked.

"I'll check this out," he promised Beth.

"Hope that means more than a phone call to

the Georgia Department of Corrections," she said stiffly. "Because that's all the Boston PD did for me."

"I told you I'd follow up. As soon as I have information, I'll call you."

The skeptical look on her face made him want to groan. Of course she had no reason to trust him, of all people. She opened her mouth, no doubt to utter some sharp retort, but her stepmother interrupted.

"Tell him about the footprints," Cynthia said.

Footprints? That was definitely more foreboding than anonymous mail. It meant danger was close by. It meant someone intended harm.

With a sigh, Beth strolled to the French doors overlooking the backyard. "Right there," she said. "They start at the tree line by the back of the property and come all the way to the patio."

A Peeping Tom, perhaps? Yet he couldn't disregard the coincidence of them appearing on the same day as the letter. He eyed the prints. Large and wide, probably from a male.

"Tell you what. I'll snap some close-up photos of these prints and follow them out to the woods. Take a look around. I'll be back shortly to collect that mail as evidence. In the meantime, don't touch it anymore, okay? The fewer fingerprints on it, the better."

"Of course," she muttered, and he had the

feeling she was barely able to refrain from rolling her eyes.

Sammy stepped outside and withdrew his cell phone, then bent on one knee and observed the footprint. About a man's size thirteen, he guessed. It wasn't much to go on. The snow was so light that no identifying shoe treads remained, only the outline of the shoe and the dark earth beneath the dusting of snow. He snapped several photos, then followed the tracks to the woods.

At the woods' edge, a *whish* sounded from behind, and he spun around.

"I wanted to see if you found anything." Beth stood before him, a stubborn set to her heart-shaped face.

It was an expression he'd witnessed several times before.

"Not a good idea. Better get back to the house, just in case. Those tracks were fresh."

"I'd rather not. And this is our property, after all. I have a right to know if anyone's trespassing."

"You also have the right to get hurt if someone's still out here," he retorted.

She said nothing, merely crossed her arms over her chest and lifted her chin a fraction. Clearly, she didn't intend to listen to reason. Especially not coming from him. He shrugged.

Whoever had been here had surely seen him pull up in the sheriff's department cruiser and had hightailed it out. "Suit yourself. But stay behind me and keep quiet."

Surprisingly, she complied. He carefully picked his way through dead vines, leafless shrubs and evergreen trees, eyes peeled for any sign of broken twigs or an object left behind. But the snow hadn't drifted down past the heavy canopy of the treetops, and there were no tracks evident, only mounds of seemingly undisturbed pine needles and twigs. Only ten feet into the woods, the ground dropped off sharply along the ridge forming Blood Mountain.

Sammy scanned the area. From here, he could view the dirt road below and the much larger Lavender Mountain, which loomed across from them. There was no evidence that anyone had recently tromped through these woods, and the unpaved road below sported an untouched sprinkling of snow. Whoever had been at the Wynngate estate was either still hiding somewhere in the thick woods, or he'd parked an ATV farther down the dirt road, well out of their sight. He stood silent for several minutes, trying to make out any unnatural rustling or spot anything out of the ordinary in the green, brown, gray and white landscape.

Nothing.

"He's gone," Beth whispered, stepping beside him.

"Appears that way. Soon as I leave here, I'll get the department's ATV and drive down the dirt road. See if there're any recent road tracks."

"You will?"

Again with the skeptical tone in her voice. "If I say I'm going to do something, I do it."

She nodded, started to turn away and then faced him again. "Thank you."

Must have killed her to say that. She clearly still held a grudge. He followed her back to the house, and just as Beth was about to reach for the patio door to reenter the den, he decided to try, one last time, to explain about that night so many years ago. He tapped her shoulder for attention and let his hand drop when she faced him.

"Look, Beth. Hear me out. I'm sorry for what happened back then. It wasn't fair that you were left taking all the blame that night for a situation that had clearly grown out of your control."

Her mouth pursed in a tight line. "Damn right it wasn't fair. The house was packed with people, and I was probably the only person in it not drinking or smoking pot."

"It was filled with *underage* people at *your* house," he reminded her. "And we found traces of heavier drugs. Not just marijuana."

"But I knew nothing about that. I didn't even know most of those people or where they came from. I was only seventeen, and somehow, a small party while my parents were away turned into something I couldn't control."

"I understood that, even as a rookie cop. But I had no—"

"I needed your help. If you understood the situation, then why the hell did you have to arrest me?"

The question hung between them.

Again he tried to explain. "Like I said, I was a rookie. My partner was an experienced patrol officer, and I was only a few weeks into my probationary period. He took the hard-nosed approach, and I had no choice in the matter."

He remembered Beth's panicked eyes that night, her tear-streaked face as she'd opened the door and let them into the house where the party raged uncontrollably. "Thank God you're here," she'd said. "I can't find Aiden anywhere."

She'd recognized him that night. He and her brother had played baseball together in the Lavender Mountain Youth League every summer for years. They'd been close friends up until high school, when Aiden had run with a different set of friends that were more into parties than sports, and they'd drifted away from each other.

"You have no idea how that arrest affected me." Beth crossed her arms and bit her lip, as though regretting that admission.

"It wasn't fair that everything came down on you," he admitted.

Sammy had no doubt Aiden was responsible for the wild crowd that evening. Yet the Golden Boy had managed to escape the debacle with no arrest record to mar his future career as a criminal attorney. Actually, everyone had gone free, save Beth. The herd of partygoers had stampeded out the back door, leaving behind all the drugs and alcohol. The quiet mountain subdivision had roared with the sound of their vehicles hastily exiting the premises.

"Forget it," she said at last, her back stiffening.

"I would, but apparently you can't," he said. "I was only doing my job that night. I hope you understand."

She gave a grudging nod. "I can appreciate that. I just wish...that you'd been able to intervene on my behalf. I was scared and unsure what to do."

That had been obvious. But Sergeant Thomas had been unmoved, ordering Sammy to handcuff Beth and place her in the cruiser.

"Did you really try to soften the older cop, or did you blindly follow orders?" Beth asked.

And there was the crux of the matter. He'd voiced his opinion, but once the sergeant shot down his objection, he'd kept his mouth shut. If he'd had it to do all over again, Sammy liked to think he'd have acted differently, have insisted that Aiden be held responsible for what had happened in that house.

He cleared his throat, about to defend himself once more, when he spotted movement within the house. Cynthia Wynngate emerged from the hallway into the den, rolling a large piece of luggage across the gleaming walnut floor.

"Does your stepmother have plans to go somewhere?" he asked.

Beth frowned and pushed open the door. "Not that I'm aware of."

They reentered the warmth of the spacious living room, where Abbie collected used coffee cups.

"Where are you going?" Beth asked Cynthia.

"Back to Atlanta. I couldn't possibly stay here after all this."

Actually, that wouldn't be a bad idea, Sammy mulled. If they left for the city, they might be safer in a new location that wasn't so isolated.

Mrs. Wynngate turned to Abbie. "I left your paycheck on the mantel. I won't be needing your services again until all this is cleared up." Her gaze flickered to where they stood by the door. "Beth, be careful about keeping the house locked tight. Officer—" her eyes scrunched as she peered at his ID badge "—Officer Armstrong. Can your department be sure to patrol by the house and keep surveillance on it? So many neighbors have already vacated their homes during the off season, and I don't want any trouble."

He blinked at the elegant woman before him. Was she really going to leave Beth behind and not even offer her the option of returning to Atlanta with her? Apparently, her only concern seemed to be for the house itself. What kind of person left another to face danger alone? Especially a family member?

Abbie spoke up. "I'll stay with you if you'd like, Beth."

"That would be great, Abbie," she said softly. "Thank you."

Mrs. Wynngate frowned. "But she's no longer in my employ."

"Abbie and I will work something out," Beth said.

He marveled at Beth's composure. Did she not even see how she'd been so coldly dismissed by her stepmother? That Cynthia had even made it clear she wasn't footing the bill for Abbie's sleepover? Or maybe this was all par for the course, and Beth expected nothing from the woman.

Strange family.

Chapter Three

Something was…not quite right.

Beth snapped from the void of sleep to alertness. Slivers of moonbeams jabbed through the blind's slats, etching vertical patterns against an onyx darkness. Although the house was silent, she was sure there had been a noise. A click of a latch, perhaps…a brief metallic ping that had no place in the dead of night.

She hardly dared move, her right hand tightly bunching a mound of down comforter as she eased into a sitting position. Seconds passed, then several minutes, the only noise a loud whooshing of her unsteady breath.

Her mind scrambled for an explanation. Maybe Abbie had awakened and gone to the bathroom down the hall, locking the door behind her. Yes, that made sense. All this business with Dorsey Lambert had troubled her so deeply that it had invaded her dreams. Yet Beth remained upright in bed, waiting for the bathroom door to creak open.

It didn't.

Cautiously, she swung her legs over the side of the bed and gently lowered her feet to the floor. Without flipping on a light, she unplugged her cell phone from the charger at her nightstand and walked to the door, her bare toes plunging into the plush carpet. Her hand grasped the doorknob, turned it ever so slowly, and then pushed the door open an inch. Just as deliberately as she'd turned the knob clockwise to open it, she released it counterclockwise and peered down the hallway.

No splinter of light shone beneath the bathroom door.

The large windows of the den's cathedral ceiling provided enough illumination to inch forward. She continued down the hallway toward the guest room at the end of the hall where Abbie was staying. At the girl's door, Beth raised a hand to knock, then hesitated. How foolish she'd look if she awakened Abbie for no reason.

Kerthunk.

Beth jumped at the sound that had emanated one story below. Her father's old study. It sounded as though one of the books had tumbled from the shelf onto the hardwood flooring. The first logical explanation that came to mind was that some nimble feline had accidently knocked over a heavy object.

Too bad Cynthia didn't have a cat.

She swallowed hard past the lump in her throat, not wanting to acknowledge the other logical conclusion: someone was in the house. Indecision tore at her. Should she call the cops and barricade herself and Abbie in the guest room, or try to figure out what the hell was going on?

The unmistakable rustling of papers from below prompted her to immediate action. She opened the bedroom door and hurried to the bed.

Abbie wasn't there.

Confusion spiked her mind. Had she entered the wrong guest room? No, the girl's overnight bag was on the dresser. So where was Abbie? Beth put a hand on her chest and willed her racing heart to slow. Now was the time for level thinking.

Perhaps Abbie was the one in the study. She'd gotten up in the middle of the night and, unable to sleep, had gone downstairs to read or watch television. She could have gone in Dad's study to get a book, accidentally bumped against the desk and knocked something over.

Beth almost smiled with relief. Still, she

kept her phone on with speed dial at the ready in case there was a more sinister explanation. She almost hadn't let Sammy put his number in her phone, but he'd appeared unwilling to leave until she allowed him to do so. And she'd wanted him to go. His presence unnerved her.

Careful to make no noise, she returned to the hallway and made her way to the winding staircase leading to the den. At the bottom of the stairs, she picked her way through the den and the kitchen. Sure enough, the study door was cracked open several inches, and dim light spilled from the lamp on Dad's desk.

She'd been right. Pleased with her logic, Beth opened her mouth to call out a greeting to Abbie, but the words died in her throat.

A man wearing jeans and a black hoodie was rifling through the file cabinet.

Not. Abbie.

He jerked a handful of papers out of a file and thrust them under the lamp, studying their contents. The intruder wore black gloves—and that detail terrified her more than the hoodie drawn tightly about his face.

She tried not to make a sound as she again picked her way back through the kitchen and then the den. Where the hell was Abbie? Beth ran up the stairs, hoping the carpet muffled her footsteps. At the top of the stairs, she paused.

She didn't dare dial Sammy, afraid the intruder would hear her speak. Instead, she shot Sammy a text: There's someone in my house.

She hit Send, and then immediately typed a second one: Hurry.

She watched until the gray bar on the text screen read Sent and then Delivered. Good. She'd follow up with a phone call once she'd locked herself in her room. But before she even reached the bedroom door, the phone vibrated in her palm. Beth waited until she was safely tucked into her room before reading the message.

On my way. Lock yourself in your room. Don't open it for anyone but me.

Thank heavens he'd responded so quickly so late at night. Yeah, she could lock herself up. But what about Abbie? She couldn't leave her to fend for herself. Beth wished she had Abbie's phone number to warn her of the danger. A sudden thought clutched at her heart: Had the intruder tied and gagged Abbie? The longer the silence, the more convinced Beth grew that it must be the case.

She padded to the window and peered through the slats. Abbie's car was still in the driveway. The girl was in as much or more danger as she was. No way Beth would cower in her room and let Abbie come to any harm. What if the intruder decided to kill her when he'd finished his business?

Before losing her courage, Beth again tiptoed out of her room. She'd grab the poker by the fireplace as a makeshift weapon. Dad used to keep a firearm in his bedroom, but she doubted Cynthia still had it. She'd always claimed that having the gun made her nervous.

Slowly, slowly, *slowly* Beth descended the stairs, vigilant for any noise or shifting patterns in the darkness. Another faint rustling of papers came from the study. At least she knew where the man was. Hastily, she scurried to the fireplace and clasped the poker. The cold, hard metal in her palms allayed her fear only an iota. If the man had a gun, the poker was useless. Still, it was better than nothing if he tried to rush at her.

She surveyed the den, seeking a bound and gagged Abbie, but the sofa and chairs were empty, and there were no signs of a struggle. Beth walked softly out of the room and went on to check the downstairs bedrooms, bathrooms and dining room. Nothing, nothing and nothing.

How much longer until Sammy arrived?

Could she have missed seeing Abbie somewhere in the kitchen? If Abbie were lucky, she'd have seen or heard the intruder and slipped outside to the patio, probably caught unawares without a phone or car keys. Even now, she might be out in the cold, shivering and frightened. First, Beth would check the kitchen, and then proceed outside.

A murmur emanated from the study, and her heart slammed in her ribs. Was the man talking to himself? More murmurs, an exchange of different pitches in the low warble of the voices.

There were *two* of them.

Her hands convulsed against the poker, and her eyes flicked around the den. A swish of fabric sounded as someone moved toward the kitchen. Whoever he was, his steps were deliberate and unhurried. She glanced over her shoulder, eyeing the distance between where she stood and the comparative safety of the hallway. It seemed to stretch as long as a football field.

No time to retreat. Beth ducked behind the sofa and prayed they were heading for the back door and leaving as quietly as they had entered.

Her nose prickled—the involuntary tingling of an oncoming sneeze. No! Not now. Fear danced in her gut. She splayed a hand across her nose and mouth, trying to suppress the telltale reflex. A muffled explosion escaped her mouth.

The fabric swishing stopped.

"What's that?" one of the men asked, his voice so near that horror chilled every inch of her flesh.

"Someone there?" another man called out.

Elliptical beams of headlights and a dizzying blue strobe pierced the glass panels lining the front door. Judging by the profusion of colors, more than one cop car had arrived at the scene.

"Damn it!"

"Let's get outta here!"

The two men raced toward the back patio and jerked open the French doors, flinging them aside. Glass exploded with a crash. Shards rained down with a loud, scattered tinkling, and a cool burst of air swept through the room, chilling her arms.

She was going to live through this nightmare. Now to find Abbie. Beth rose, still clutching the poker. "Abbie?" she called. "It's safe now. Where are you?"

A high-pitched cry exploded through the open patio door. Abbie was alive.

Beth ran forward. "Abbie? You all right?"

Abbie ran in the door, her red hair sprinkled with snow and her arms clasped around her waist. Blood dribbled from a cut in her forehead, and she shivered violently.

"They hurt you!" Beth cried. She grabbed a woolen afghan from the sofa and draped it over Abbie's shoulders. "You must be freezing. You're safe now. Let the cops in the front door while I lock the patio doors."

Outside, the stygian atmosphere wholly absorbed any sight of the trespassers. The intruders' dark clothing had allowed them to slip into the black velvet of the night. Hastily, she pulled the door shut and fastened the lock. More glass splintered and crashed to the floor. One good kick and the whole glass door would completely shatter. Hardly did any good to secure it shut, but maybe it would buy a few seconds' time if the intruders returned and had to kick the remaining glass.

"Beth! Are you okay?"

She swiveled at Sammy's shout, surprised at its underlying sound of concern.

"We're good," she called.

He entered the den, his eyes immediately fixating on her face. She pointed at the door. "They ran outside."

Footsteps trampled in the hallway as more officers entered. Sirens blared, signaling that more were on the way. Beth rubbed her arms, suddenly conscious she was clad in an old T-shirt and pajama bottoms.

Sammy stood beside her, draped a blanket over her shoulders and wordlessly guided her to the sofa. Abbie was already seated nearby, speaking with an officer.

His kind brown eyes calmed her as he waited, letting her catch her breath. Old memories suddenly resurfaced. Instead of seeing Sammy as an emblem of the great divide in her life that had spiraled her fortune downward, Beth remembered her teenage crush on him. He was Aiden's close friend, several years older and totally out of reach. During their summers at Blood Mountain, she'd attended every baseball game he and Aiden played, secretly thrilling at his muscular physique in uniform, the speed with which he ran bases, the skill and power with which he batted.

The house suddenly blazed with swirling blue lights from every window. Out back, a floodlight flicked on and illuminated the yard all the way to the mountain ridge. The rooms buzzed with the cackle of two-way radios and men shouting orders as they spread through the house, guns drawn. Beth dropped her gaze from Sammy, pushing the memories away. "Thanks for getting here so quickly."

"I told you to call whenever you needed me. I'm glad you did."

She looked back up, studying the gentle and determined set of his face. The chaos surrounding them melted away, and only his dark eyes remained. For the first time all day, she felt warm and safe.

Until he opened his mouth.

"How well do you know this Abbie girl?"

She shrugged, surprised at the question. "Well enough, I guess. She's worked two or three years for Cynthia, and we've talked a bit during my brief visits. She works part-time here and goes to community college. Why? What about her?"

"Do you even know her last name?"

Sheepish, Beth glanced down at her bare feet. "Honestly, no. But what does that matter? She's always—"

"It matters plenty," he cut in, his tone rough with suspicion.

Beth gave Abbie a quick glance. The girl's forehead was already beginning to swell and bruise. Someone had handed her a tissue, and she blotted at the trickle of blood still seeping from her wound. Beth already sensed Sammy's answer, but she had to ask anyway. "What's Abbie's last name?" she whispered.

"It's Lambert."

Chapter Four

"Lambert?" Beth's body recoiled in surprise.

Pretty much his reaction when he'd checked up on the girl this afternoon. "Actually, it's her maiden name. But yeah."

"She doesn't look old enough to be married." Beth studied Abbie from across the room.

"Married at seventeen, divorced at twenty-one. Legal name is Abigail Lambert Fenton."

"I had no idea. Cynthia couldn't have known that either when she hired her."

"To be fair, Lambert's a common name in these hills. Dorsey was originally from Ellijay, only thirty miles from here. Man's got plenty of extended family in the area."

"Seems I ran straight into the lion's den," Beth said with a snort. "Should have stayed in Boston."

"Could be her relationship to Dorsey is distant, and this is all a coincidence." Not that Sammy believed that for a minute. Abbie Fenton was probably involved up to her freckled little neck in this mischief. With any luck, he'd put a stop to it all this evening. No more threats and break-ins.

"She seemed so nice." Hurt chased across Beth's eyes.

"You know what they say. Got to watch those quiet ones," he said, attempting a smile to alleviate her worry. "Woman even volunteered to stay the night with you. Call me jaded, but that rang an alarm in my mind. I'd intended to come back this morning and have a chat with her. Imagine my surprise when I got your text."

Beth's gray eyes widened. "You don't think she had anything to do with those intruders, do you? I mean, she's hurt."

"A superficial cut on the forehead. Could be self-induced. And at first glance, I see no signs of forced entry. Officers are checking all the windows and doors as we speak."

"Surely you don't think… Are you saying Abbie *let* them in?"

"We're not ruling anything out at this point. Now tell me everything that happened tonight. What first alerted you—"

Beth shoved the chair from beneath her and strode to where Abbie sat with an officer. The woman's mouth opened in surprise when she spotted Beth headed her way. Abbie's eyes hardened, and she stiffly drew up her slight frame, clearly signaling she expected a confrontation and was prepared to dig in her heels.

"Did you let those men in my house?" Beth asked, voice tight with anger.

A sullen Abigail lifted her chin and refused to respond. She looked older now, a certain sternness in her features that hadn't been there earlier. Officer Graham raised a quizzical brow at Sammy.

Quickly, Sammy rushed to Beth's side. "Let us ask the questions," he admonished.

Beth ignored him. "Well, did you?" she persisted. "Why? What do they want?"

Abbie kept her face averted, eyes focused on the patio door, her mouth set in a grim twist.

Sammy took Beth's elbow and steered her to the kitchen. Beth still wasn't through. "How could you do such a thing?" she called over her shoulder. "We trusted you!"

"Let Officer Graham ask the questions and do his job. In the meantime, I want a statement from you."

"Can I at least put on a sweater and start coffee?" she grumbled.

"Be my guest." There was no hurry. He'd stay here all night if necessary. He wouldn't rest until the intruders had been found and Abbie had confessed to her role in tonight's invasion.

More important, he wouldn't leave Beth alone in this house until he knew she was safe.

She hurried from the kitchen, nearly colliding with Officer Markwell. Both officers watched as she slipped from the room.

"No signs of forced entry anywhere," Markwell reported without preamble. "No open or broken windows, no damaged doors and no footprints around the sides of the house. Point of entry appears to be the patio door, where we found several sets of footprints leading to the woods at the back of the property."

"No damage to the patio door locks?" he asked.

"None."

The two-way radio at his belt crackled, and the voice of Officer Lipscomb cut in. "No sign yet of anyone on the property. Heading to the road below to see if there are any tracks."

"Ten-four," he answered before turning to Markwell. "Sweep through every room. Make sure they're empty and mark any signs of disturbance."

Markwell left, and Sammy stared at Abbie. Her lips were pinched together, and her chin lifted in stubborn defiance. She was going to be a tough nut to crack.

Beth reentered the kitchen wearing a long, loose cardigan sweater. She'd also donned a pair of thick woolen socks. Without sparing him a glance, she poured water into the coffee maker. "Want a cup?" she asked, her back to him.

"No, but I'll take a soda if you've got one."

"In the fridge. Help yourself."

He got out a can and opened it, taking a long swallow as he watched Beth. Her hands trembled as she pressed the machine's buttons. Now that the shock had worn off, the reality of what had happened was settling in. He'd seen it many times before.

"We won't leave until we're sure your place is locked up tight," he assured her. "And we'll keep a patrol outside, too."

She looked up, and her lips trembled before she offered a tight smile. "Thank you. Really. I don't know what might have happened if you hadn't arrived so quickly."

For the first time in ages, Beth gazed at him without a trace of acrimony. The air between them crackled with an electrical charge, one not caused by animosity. That was certainly new.

The aroma of coffee filled the air, and she jerked her gaze away, busying herself with retrieving a cup from the cabinet. After she'd fortified her nerves with the brew, he'd walk with Beth to the downstairs study and ask her to check for any missing items.

What had those men been after? This went way beyond the scare tactics of menacing mail. And if it had been a robbery, they would have gone after electronics or searched for jewelry and money. Beth's purse hung on the back of one of the kitchen chairs, apparently undisturbed.

"Check your bag," he said. "See if anything's missing."

Beth gasped and went to her purse. "Didn't even think of that." After riffling through it and opening her wallet, she shook her head. "Everything's here—my credit cards, cash and driver's license."

No simple burglary, then. Of course, he'd known that anyway because of Abbie's obvious connection with the Lambert clan. But what had they been after? Again, his gaze drifted to the recalcitrant, unremorseful Abigail. Doubtful she was going to volunteer any information.

Did she and other members of Dorsey's disreputable family really believe that Judge Wynngate had been corrupt? Had they planned tonight's invasion to search for evidence to back their wild claims?

It was the only explanation that made sense. As Beth sipped coffee, he strolled to the kitchen window, watching snowflakes sift quietly to the ground. Had the men found what they'd come to collect? Would they return? If they did, it would be incredibly stupid, but no one said criminals possessed the brightest brains.

Returning would be a grave mistake on their part. There'd be no more Abbie to silently open the door and allow them easy access. Still, he should probably convince Beth that she wasn't safe here, that the best thing she could do was return to Boston as soon as possible. At the very least, she needed to spend the rest of her visit with her stepmother in Atlanta—whether Cynthia Wynngate wanted her there or not.

Sammy quashed the small dash of disappointment that arose at the prospect of Beth leaving. She intrigued him, even all those years ago when she'd sat in the stands watching him and Aiden playing baseball. But their age difference had seemed too great then, and she was his friend's sister, after all. Back then, Aiden's friendship had been important to him. Aiden... a solution popped into his mind.

"Maybe it's time you paid a visit to Aiden," he suggested. "At least until we've made an arrest and it's safe to return. How long were you planning to stay on vacation, anyway?"

She lifted a shoulder and let it drop. "No idea. I like to play things by ear. Keep it fluid. I'm free until after the New Year, when classes start up again. I teach art to middle schoolers."

Aiden had mentioned that Beth had an "artsy" job teaching children. He'd said it with a smile that Sammy couldn't decipher, either proud of his sister's occupation or indulgent in a patronizing way.

"So what about visiting your brother?" he asked again, aware she'd sidestepped the question.

She lifted the cup to her lips and took a small sip before answering. "Maybe."

He didn't push. His peripheral vision picked up Officer Graham motioning to him. Sammy started in his direction, and Graham met him halfway.

"The suspect's refusing to answer questions. How about I take her to the station?"

A change of environment might loosen her tongue, especially when faced with the chill starkness of an interrogation room. Members of the Lambert family were no strangers to a jail's ambience, but perhaps Abbie was young enough never to have witnessed it outside of family visitation days. Being questioned and held in a cell didn't compare to the inmate guest experience.

"Yep. Get her out of here," he told Graham. "And don't release her unless you check with me first."

Graham returned to the den, took Abbie by

the arm and guided her toward the foyer. She pointedly kept her face averted to avoid Sammy's gaze. Or Beth's. Either way, Sammy took it as a sign of guilt. If Abbie were innocent, she'd be pleading her case to Beth.

"Glad she's gone," Beth muttered. "I hope to never see her again."

"You won't have to. Next time, Cynthia needs to be more thorough in hiring help."

"Agreed." Beth set down her cup. "Ready to take my statement?"

"First, let's go to your dad's office. Take a good look around and see if anything's missing."

Beth tugged the sweater and gave a brisk nod. Wordlessly, she strode past him, and he followed her through the main floor and then down one level to the study.

The room was brightly lit from an overhead fixture as well as a lamp atop a huge mahogany desk. Two matching mahogany file cabinets, most of the drawers hanging open, banked a side wall. Behind the desk, legal tomes crammed a floor-to-ceiling bookcase. A steady, studious office with an old-fashioned vibe. All befitting a judge.

Several files were scattered across the desk's gleaming surface, along with an open laptop. Papers littered the floor where the intruders had dropped them in their haste to leave. Without touching the papers, Sammy leaned down to peer at the words. Seemed to be court records of various convicted felons. He put on a pair of plastic gloves, and with the tip of a finger, he turned the computer to face him. The screen was black. He tapped the keyboard, and a desktop wallpaper featuring the Atlanta federal courthouse sprang to life. In the center of the monitor was:

Edward Preston Wynngate III
Invalid Password. Try again.

The intruders hadn't cracked the code, so they weren't dealing with experienced hackers. Sammy wondered if they'd planned on stealing the laptop to investigate further, but the unexpected arrival of the cops had interrupted their plan. "Do you know your father's password?" he asked Beth.

She shook her head. "Sorry. He was a reserved man and preferred we not even enter his office while he was working. Said it disturbed his concentration." Her eyes scanned the room. "Actually, he didn't like people coming in even when he wasn't at work."

"Why?"

"He was very meticulous. Probably afraid we'd mess everything up."

Sammy could think of another reason. One

that had to do with keeping secrets. "To your knowledge, does Cynthia ever use this computer?"

"I doubt it. She prefers to do everything either on her phone or tablet."

Then Mrs. Wynngate should have no objections to them temporarily confiscating the laptop and having a computer forensic expert review its contents. The sooner they got to the bottom of what Dorsey Lambert was seeking, the safer the Wynngate family would be. Sammy made a mental note to call her first thing in the morning.

"Take a good look around," he urged Beth. "Anything valuable your father kept down here?"

"Not that I'm aware of. But like I said, it isn't a place I entered very often."

He skirted around to the back of the desk and opened a few drawers. Nothing but standard office supplies, neatly arranged and stacked.

His mind flashed to his infrequent meetings with the judge over the years. The man had been physically fit for his age and pleasant enough. But something about his rigid stance, even in the comfort of his home, and his meticulous formality had been off-putting to Sammy—as though with a glance, the judge had taken stock of Sammy's blue-collar background and had merely tolerated him as Aiden's temporary buddy in the weeks they lived at Falling Rock each summer.

Beth sank onto the desk chair and groaned, placing her head in her hands. "What do these lunatic Lamberts want?"

Proof. The answer sprang into his mind fully formed, pure and simple. They must believe Lambert was unfairly sentenced and were out to avenge the family name. Had there been anything shady behind the conviction on the judge's end? He'd question Beth as tactfully as possible.

"Any possibility your father might be involved in something unethical?"

Her head snapped up, and she glared. "Dad was beyond reproach. The most ethical person you'd ever meet. You could even describe him as unyielding when it came to his principles. Maybe too rigid."

Her eyes grew unfocused as she strummed her fingers on the polished mahogany. Obviously, her thoughts had drifted away from the present situation. Sammy could well imagine the judge as a stern, remote father who imposed a strict code of justice. He'd never particularly cared for the guy, but he pushed aside his personal feelings. Had Judge Wynngate truly been on the take or involved in criminal activity?

Dorsey Lambert sure held a grudge against the man. He'd have a talk with him and ask what he, or his family, believed the judge might have in his office and why they'd sent Beth threatening mail. Bad enough she'd been the one left holding the bag when Aiden and his buddies had disappeared from that ill-fated party years ago. Hadn't she already suffered enough for a family member's transgression?

He wouldn't let it happen again.

"Do you have somewhere to stay tonight?" Sammy asked, breaking her reverie. "A friend you can stay with? At the very least, you could drive to Atlanta and stay with Aiden for the time being. I'm sure he—"

"I'm not calling him at this time of night," she answered stiffly. Clearly, Beth was still rankled over his earlier remark about her father.

"I don't want to leave you alone here with the broken door."

She rose and brushed past him. "Of course I won't stay here tonight. I'll go to a motel until I figure out what to do in the morning."

"Good plan. I'll drive you over."

Her gray eyes bore into him. "You've done enough. I'm perfectly capable of driving myself."

Seems when it came to Beth Wynngate, he just couldn't win.

Chapter Five

Sammy's question about her father's integrity pricked Beth's heart like barbed wire. If he'd known her father, he'd never doubt the man's honesty and rigid moral code. Her spoon clanked so loudly against her cup she was surprised other customers at the coffee shop didn't glance her way.

Bells tinkled, and a gust of cold air whipped through the room as the door opened. Lilah Sampson walked in, golden curls enveloping her in an angelic aura. People craned their necks to catch a glimpse of her, their eyes softening and mouths involuntarily upturning at the fresh cheerfulness she naturally bestowed upon everyone. Lilah scanned the shop and then waved at Beth, hurrying over to her table.

"Hey, Beth! It's good to see you again." Lilah gave her a quick embrace, her pregnant belly bumping into Beth's abs. Lilah released her and awkwardly dropped onto the opposite chair, hands gripping the table for balance.

"You look so happy. And healthy," Beth said. Pregnancy certainly agreed with her old friend.

"I'm both of the above," Lilah agreed. "Although sometimes I wonder how I'm ever going to take care of a new baby when Ellie is a little hellion."

"How old is she again? Two? Three?"

"Almost four years old." Lilah extracted her cell phone from her purse. "Just one quick picture, I promise."

Dutifully, Beth cooed over the photo of the blue-eyed blonde—which was easy to do, as Ellie was an adorable mini version of her mother. "Here," she said, pushing the plate of doughnuts toward Lilah. "Chocolate frosting with sprinkles."

"My fave. I shouldn't, but I can never say no to them. Especially now." Lilah picked up a doughnut, brought it halfway to her mouth and then stopped. She set it back down, her face tight with concern. "The smell of chocolate in this place must have scrambled my brains. How are you? I mean, I know what happened at your place yesterday."

"Figured Harlan would fill you in." As sheriff, her husband had a pulse on everything that went down in Elmore County.

"I wish he'd told me last night instead of waiting until this morning. Why didn't you call? You know you can stay with me until you need to go back to Boston."

She loved her old friend but staying with her for more than a day or two was out of the question. Lilah kept busy enough with her own family and work without an additional burden. "I stayed at a motel last night. I'll probably go visit Aiden a few days. But first, I want to oversee getting the patio doors fixed this afternoon. Cynthia would have a fit if she knew they were busted."

Lilah's eyes flashed confusion. "You mean she doesn't know about the break-in yet? Thought you would have called her immediately."

"There was no point worrying her so late in the evening. Nothing was stolen. Guess I should run it by her, though, if Sammy hasn't already told her about it. Cynthia needs to be careful not to hire any more Lamberts."

Lilah shrugged, and her mouth ticked upward in a wan smile. "The Lamberts are the only family whose name has a worse reputation around here than the Tedders."

The Tedders were infamous moonshiners and outlaws. Their penchant for crime had even become national news four years earlier. Still, as far as Beth was concerned, Lilah's brush with a serial killer in her family was worse than her own scare the previous night. "But you're not a Tedder anymore," Beth reminded her. "You're a Sampson."

"Ha! As if anyone in Lavender Mountain's going to forget my maiden name." But Lilah smiled and took a bite of her doughnut as though she couldn't care less about other people's opinions. Harlan Sampson might not be Beth's cup of tea, but he made Lilah happy, and that was all that mattered.

"Bet Cynthia hasn't forgotten my background," Lilah said with a roll of her eyes.

Beth's stepmother had never approved of her friendship with, as she put it, "that Tedder girl." But surprisingly, her father had overruled his wife, saying that Beth needed a friend during the summers spent at Blood Mountain. And Lilah had been a true friend. Their friendship had remained strong even after Beth had been exiled to a private school for troubled rich kids. Beth would never forget Lilah's kindness, especially since her former friends at the elite Atlanta academy where she'd attended high school regarded her as a social pariah. She'd never heard from any of them again.

"The important people in our lives don't care about our past," Beth reminded Lilah. A current of understanding bolted through the short distance between them. If they lived to be a hundred, they'd always have this bond.

Lilah bit into the doughnut again and momentarily closed her eyes, apparently blissed out on sugar. Guilt nibbled in Beth's stomach. She hadn't invited Lilah over for a casual chat. Best to just ask the favor and get it over with. "How much did Harlan tell you about last night?" she asked.

Lilah's eyes flew open. "Everything," she admitted. "Hope you don't mind. He knows we're close, and I'd want to hear it from him before anyone else."

"Even about…the possible motive behind the break-in?" Sammy's question about her father still stung.

"Yeah," Lilah nodded. "They have to explore every angle and ask the tough questions. Part of the job."

Beth tamped down her reluctance to ask for the favor. Was she as bad as Cynthia, expecting to get preferential treatment because of her social status? No, she decided. This was merely a request from one friend to another. Cynthia wouldn't ask—she'd demand. She wasn't anything like her stepmother. Beth went out of her way not to flaunt her name or her money. Her only motive in asking the favor was to keep

Sammy at arm's length. Besides questioning her father's character, he brought up too many memories and made her uncomfortable. She drew a deep breath and then blurted, "Is there any way Harlan can oversee the investigation?"

"You mean, instead of Sammy?"

"Exactly."

Lilah cocked her head to the side. "Harlan's involved in a big case right now with the Georgia Bureau of Investigation. It eats up all his time."

Disappointment seeped into her. At least she'd tried.

"What's the problem?" Lilah asked. "Sammy's his right-hand man. Besides, have you met Sammy's partner, Charlotte?"

"No. She wasn't there last night."

"Well, Charlotte's great. She used to work for the Atlanta PD and has lots of experience. They'll get to the bottom of the case."

A wry voice beside them cut through their conversation. "Thanks for the vote of confidence."

Beth almost jumped at the sight of the officer who glared down at her, clutching a white bag of pastries. The buttons of her brown uniform blouse stretched tightly across her heavily pregnant belly, threatening to pop open at any moment. Her red hair was pulled back in a ponytail, and her eyes stared accusingly at Beth.

"You don't get to decide which officer investigates which case," the fierce redhead said stiffly.

Lilah quickly tried to defuse the situation. "Beth, this is my sister-in-law, Charlotte. Sammy's partner." She flashed a placating smile at Charlotte. "We were just talking about the break-in."

But Charlotte ignored Lilah and kept her gaze directed at Beth. She read the woman's name badge: C. Tedder. What rotten luck that she happened to be walking by at the exact moment she'd asked Lilah for a favor. Beth had forgotten how frequently this kind of chance encounter could occur in a small town.

"I assure you that your case will receive due diligence on our part," Officer Tedder said in a clipped voice.

"Good to know," Beth muttered.

"You have any complaint with the way we're conducting our investigation?"

The woman was relentless. Determined to put her in her place. "Not yet," she mumbled.

"Charlotte and Sammy are the best," Lilah said easily. "What flavor doughnuts did you get?" she asked her sister-in-law in an obvious attempt to change the subject.

Charlotte answered, keeping her gaze affixed on Beth, "Lemon custard."

A sour treat for a sour cop. But Beth didn't dare say it aloud. At last Charlotte broke eye contact and regarded Lilah. The stern set of her jaw softened as she gave her a small nod. With a start, Beth realized the woman was actually pretty when she wasn't being such a hard-ass.

"See you at dinner this evening?" the woman asked. "James plans to grill steaks."

"Wouldn't miss it."

With one final glare in Beth's direction, Charlotte eased away from their table.

"Whew." Beth let out a sigh as she watched Charlotte exit the building. "I'm not winning friends and influencing people today, am I?" she joked.

Lilah merely laughed. "She'll get over it. Maybe we can all have lunch together one day."

She'd as soon have dental surgery than endure a meal with Officer Tedder. But it was too late to do any good, so Beth kept her mouth shut. No need to alienate anyone else affiliated with the sheriff's office. Poor James. What must it be like for Lilah's brother, married to a woman like that? Beth sighed, resigned now to having Sammy and Charlotte as the investigators of record. She wouldn't be around much longer, anyway, so no big deal. Might as well enjoy time with her friend while she had the opportunity. The rest of her get-together with Lilah was pleasant, as Beth put the encounter with Charlotte behind her.

Thirty minutes later, bundled against the winter chill, Beth returned to her car. She kept her head bent low, away from the full force of the biting wind. A pair of large men's boots beneath two tall columns of denim suddenly appeared in her view, and she moved to the right to get out of the way.

A large hand clamped on her right forearm. Startled, she stared up at a giant of a man. He glared, blue eyes lasering through the frosty air. Thick red hair curled out beneath his knitted hat, and a scarf covered his chin and mouth. A muffled, guttural sound tried to escape the woolen scarf.

"What are you doing? Let go of me," she snapped, trying to snatch her arm from his grasp. He tightened it several degrees. Even through the thick coat, his fingers dug painfully into her flesh. Where was grumpy Officer Charlotte Tedder when she actually needed her? Beth scanned the practically vacant street. Nowhere, evidently. *Figures*.

The stranger lowered his scarf and growled. "You owe us."

What the hell did that mean? Was he a bill

collector? All her bills were paid. Maybe he had her confused with someone else. "Are you a car repossesser or something? You must be mistaken. Now let go of me before I start screaming."

"Ain't no mistake, Elizabeth Jane Wynngate. Pay us back the fifty grand, and we'll go away."

"Fifty grand?" She practically snorted in derision. "Let me just get my checkbook out of my purse." His demand ricocheted in her brain. "Wait a minute. *Us? Who is us?*" And then she understood.

"That's right," he nodded, evidently seeing the light dawn in her eyes.

"Are you Dorsey in the flesh or another family member ordered to harass me?" She'd guess family member. From what she'd seen in the news media years ago, Dorsey had been a short, thin man with skinny wrists and ankles. His prison uniform practically fell off his small frame as he'd been led from a Department of Corrections van into a federal court building.

Her father's courtroom.

"We only want what's due us," he said gruffly. "Play fair."

"Your due for what? You think it's fair to intimidate me into giving you my money? Extortion's a serious crime. I'm not paying a dime just to get you off my back. Leave me alone before I call the cops on you."

The fingers on her arm loosened. With his free hand, the man dug into his coat pocket and pulled out a slip of paper. "Get the cash. By tomorrow evening. Then call this number, and we'll come collect." With a gloved hand, he thrust the paper into her palm. "Don't be stupid. The number goes to a burner phone. And no matter where you go, remember, we're watching you."

He pivoted and, with surprising speed for a man his size, hurried down the alley adjoining the coffee shop and an antique store. Beth glanced down at his large footprints in the snow. Was he one of the same men who'd been sneaking around their property? Maybe he was even one of the masked intruders who'd eluded the law last evening.

Anger overcame her fear. Perhaps if she followed him, she could get his car tag or another clue for the police to find him and bring him in for questioning. Quickly, she raced to her car and started the engine. If she hurried, there was a chance she could make it around the block and onto the street running parallel before he got away. Beth accelerated from the curb, thankful that the streets were practically empty. At the stop sign twenty yards ahead, she barely slowed as she turned right and then took an immediate left.

Ahead, she spotted the Lambert family member hopping into a rusty pickup truck and speeding off as fast as the old engine allowed. Without stopping to examine the risk, Beth hit the accelerator on her sleek sports car. If it came to a speed race, she'd be the clear winner. If nothing else, she had the make and model of his vehicle now. But if she could draw a little closer, she'd get the real prize—a tag number.

Beth pulled up Sammy's number on her Bluetooth dashboard and punched the button. It rang over and over. His deep, disembodied voice sounded. "Sorry, I'm unable to come to the phone right now. At the tone, please leave a message, or if this is an emergency, please call 911."

She smashed a palm on the dashboard. Where the hell was he? She didn't let up on the gas as the truck she followed left town and turned onto a county road, its wheels screeching in the haste to put distance between them. They both began their ascent up Lavender Mountain. The road narrowed and twisted up the steep incline.

Finally, *finally* the voice recording ended with a loud, drawn-out beep.

"Sammy? It's me. Beth. I was harassed in

town today by someone sent by Dorsey. I'm following his truck now. It's a rusted-out blue Ford. And the tag number is…" She squinted her eyes. The sun reflecting off the white snow was almost blinding. "It's GA 9—"

A cannonade sound erupted, followed by a steep drop on the right side of her car. Her vehicle swerved, and she gripped the steering wheel, praying she didn't spin out of control down the side of the mountain. The entire right side of her car swiped the flimsy guardrail, the metal screech ringing in her ears. At the last possible second, Beth righted the vehicle's course. A sharp pain bulldozed down her back at the whiplash movement. What had she run over that had flattened her tire and caused so much damage? The truck driver leaned out of the open window on the driver's side and leveled a shotgun.

Oh, hell. That explained everything. The first shot had blown out a tire. Was she the next target?

Beth slumped beneath the dashboard and hit the brakes. Her car skidded on the icy road.

Boom.

The BMW dropped a foot on the left side. The man had shot out her other front tire. She couldn't stay behind the dashboard any longer with her car spinning out of control. Death could as easily come from a crash off the mountain as a bullet. Beth rose up and managed to bring her car to a complete stop. The muscle pull in her back spasmed, and she caught her breath, forcing her lungs to take in oxygen more slowly and shallowly.

The blue truck rounded a bend in the road and passed out of sight. She supposed she should be thankful he didn't hop out of the truck with his shotgun and approach. But he wasn't trying to kill her. Not yet, anyway. He—they—wanted her money, and that meant keeping her alive.

But what if he came back anyway? This could be a chance to kidnap her and force her to withdraw money from an ATM or write a check. She needed the cops. Beth inserted the car key into the lock, but it wouldn't turn. Something had jammed the ignition. Okay, then. Her car was dead, but she still had her cell phone to call for help.

Only…where had it gone? Frantically, her gaze roamed the floorboards, but it wasn't there. She reached behind her to pat her seat, but the movement shot another burst of pain through her spine. She groaned, more in frustration than from the hurt. The phone had to be there somewhere. Steeling herself, she gingerly scooted forward, then extended her arm backward, but her hand only brushed against the smooth leather seats. She really didn't want to do this, but the alternative was to remain where she was—a sitting duck if the man returned. For all she knew, he might have collected one or two more of his family to come kidnap her and do Lord knows what.

Cautiously she reached a hand under the driver's seat. She gasped; a sharp knife of pain shot through her as her back protested the movement. Her vision went dark, and she collapsed forward. Deep, deep breaths. Her sight might have forsaken her, but she could hear the wind in the trees, the far-off sound of cars in town. She'd read once that your hearing was the last thing to go before unconsciousness. Unfortunately, she now knew it to be true.

Everything's going to be all right, she repeated to herself like a mantra. Someone was bound to be along this road shortly. They'd call the police. Sammy would find her. And probably be furious that she'd been so foolish as to chase after a man who'd threatened her. She deserved a scolding, too, not that she'd admit such a thing.

And then she heard it. The roar of a vehicle approaching. The direction the noise came from was in front of her, which meant the person was descending the mountain. It wasn't someone from town climbing back up. The abrupt squeal of brakes rang out, and then a door opened and slammed shut.

Blood pounded in her ears, and she hardly dared try to lift her head and open her eyes. Good chance that whoever approached might be her tormentor and not her savior. Heavy footsteps crunched through snow and came to an abrupt halt by her car. She feared that if she opened her eyes, she'd find an enemy within a couple of feet of where she slumped, easy prey for the taking.

Chapter Six

From the corner of his eyes, Sammy caught Charlotte waving at him. He pushed away from his desk and crossed the aisle where she sat, phone glued to an ear. *Lambert*, she mouthed.

He plopped into the metal chair beside his partner, eavesdropping. He'd tried several times that morning to make contact with the forwarding phone number on file for Dorsey Lambert. No one had answered his call, and despite his repeated message that it was urgent they speak, they hadn't bothered to call back, either.

"Yes, Mrs. Lambert. Good to hear your son's found a job and is staying out of trouble," Charlotte said in her most soothing tone. She flashed him a wink. "There's no problem that a simple conversation with Dorsey wouldn't clear up. When do you expect him home this evening?"

A long pause.

"I promise we're not out to fling him back in jail if he's staying clean. We've got a little matter in Elmore County that we believe he can help us with, that's all."

Charlotte held up crossed fingers at him, and he returned the gesture. With any luck, they'd get answers from the ex-convict tonight.

"Seven o'clock tonight is perfect. Yes, ma'am. And thank you."

She hung up the phone and gave a satisfied smirk. "Mama Lambert is convinced her son is a new man. Prison reformed his sorry ass."

Sadly, he shared her cynical outlook. He'd seen the recidivism rates on felons, and recent circumstances had done nothing to make him believe Dorsey Lambert was going to prove an exception to those abysmal statistics.

Charlotte's two-way radio emitted a loud crackle, and she unclipped it from her belt. Sammy glanced down at the desk blotter and read the scribbled address for Rayna Clementine Lambert. Ellijay would be a short trip. He'd contact Sheriff Roby in Gilmer County beforehand as a professional courtesy.

"Ten-ten at the Flight Club," Charlotte announced abruptly, standing and then quickly heading to the station exit.

"This early in the day?" He shook his head as he leaped to his feet and followed on her heels. "Where's Graham and Markwell? They can take this call."

He didn't say what he was really thinking. If he did, Charlotte would give him a good blistering for trying to protect her. Despite starting maternity leave in a couple of weeks, she refused to ask for special accommodations and insisted on carrying out business as usual. Her husband, James, had given up trying to convince her to take the temporary desk job Sammy had offered.

Despite her stubbornness, Sammy had to admit she was the best partner he'd ever had. He worried she wouldn't want to return to the job after her maternity leave was over, but she'd assured him otherwise.

With an efficiency born of a long working relationship, Charlotte proceeded to the driver's side of the cruiser—it was her turn to drive—while he slipped into the passenger seat. She flicked on the blue lights, and they pulled out of the station.

"Who you reckon it's going to be this time?" he asked. "The Halbert brothers?"

"My money's on Ike Johnson starting up trouble again."

"Usual bet?" he asked.

"You're on."

She sped through the main street intersection and onto the county road heading south. The Flight Club was less than two miles down the road, an ugly concrete square of a building with a dirt parking lot always filled with worse-for-the-wear vehicles, no matter the time of day or night.

A roll of unease rumbled through his gut as they pulled up to the building, the way it always did whenever he caught sight of the run-down bar. As a teenager, he'd spent way too many evenings here coaxing his inebriated father to get in his car so he could drive him home.

Before they exited the cruiser, two men tumbled out the front door, each grabbing a shirtful of the other as they dragged their fight outside. Bert Fierra, the club's owner and bartender, stood in the doorway, scowling at the men.

"The Halbert brothers," Sammy said to Charlotte as they approached the fighters. "You owe me. I'll take Hank while you take Charlie."

She shot him a suspicious look. Charlie was the smaller of the two brothers. Lucky for him, there was no time for her to argue that she was capable of taking on the bigger guy.

Within minutes, they had the two separated, hands cuffed behind their backs and inside the cruiser. Both were too drunk to offer much resistance. As was their habit, the two brothers quickly made up and were contrite by the time they'd reached the station and been placed in lockup.

"Not only do you owe me a six-pack of soda, you get to handle the paperwork," he told Charlotte smugly once they returned to their desks.

"I can finish it in half the time it takes you," she bragged.

"Then you should file the incident reports every time."

"You wish."

"A guy can try." Sammy chuckled as he slid into his seat. "We make a good team."

She slid him a sly glance. "Too bad Beth Wynngate doesn't appreciate our awesomeness."

His amusement melted. "What do you mean?"

"Overheard her talking to Lilah this morning at the doughnut shop. Seems she wants to pull the friendship card and get Harlan to take over the case."

Surprise, then resentment, flushed over him. "Did she say why?"

"Isn't it obvious? She must hold our investigative skills in low regard."

Either that, or Beth was still put out that he'd questioned the judge's possible involvement in something unethical or illegal. "What did Lilah say?"

"Basically, that Harlan was too busy at the moment and that she should trust us."

"Bet that thrilled her." If Beth was anything like Cynthia, she'd keep demanding until she had her way. Sammy tried to let the insult roll off his shoulders, but found it surprisingly difficult.

He dug his cell phone from his jacket pocket and laid it on the desk. Missed call. Voice mail message lit up the screen. In the bustle of taking in the Halberts, he hadn't noticed the phone ringing. He tapped Play on the voice mail app, and Beth's voice, tinny with excitement and fear, spilled into his ears. His chest tightened as he listened and then nearly burst at the unmistakable crack of a bullet erupting. Had Lambert found her? Or had he sent a hit man? Tires squealed on the road. The message played on in eerie silence for thirty seconds before the recording ended.

"Damn it!" He slammed his hand on the desk. What had happened? Where was she now? He checked the time of the recording: 10:18 a.m., almost ten minutes since she'd dialed.

Charlotte quirked a brow. "What's up?"

"Check with the dispatcher. See what calls have come through in the last fifteen minutes."

Charlotte grabbed her phone while he dialed her number. Beth's cell phone rang three times before switching to voice mail. He dialed again.

And again. He dug the cruiser keys from his pocket. If nothing else, he'd drive out toward Falling Rock to see if there'd been any accidents. If she were alone and injured, or in grave peril, he had to find her. At once.

"A ten-fifty-two call came in less than a minute ago," Charlotte announced. "Fuller's en route."

An ambulance request? Sammy raced to the front door as Charlotte followed at his heels, passing along more information.

"Address given was County Road 190, about a third the way up Lavender Mountain. A citizen reported a green BMW Z3 blocking the road. A woman was slumped over the dashboard and unresponsive."

Beth's car. The tightness in his chest twisted deeper, squeezing his lungs. Had she been shot? Sammy's mind whirled as he got in their cruiser, Charlotte beside him, and peeled out of the station and toward the accident scene.

"What's going on?" Charlotte asked.

He nodded at his cell phone on the console. "Play the last voice mail."

Charlotte did. Again the crack of a bullet and squealing tires ripped into him, doubling his tension.

At last they turned onto the county road. A police sedan was ahead of them, lights flashing and siren blaring. Sammy hit the gas until he nearly overtook Officer Fuller responding to the call. From behind, the wail of an ambulance sounded.

"Don't get us wrecked trying to assist Fuller," Charlotte warned. "You're no good to Beth hurt."

But he could think of nothing except Beth needing him at once. If Lambert had managed to get to her, this was his fault. He should have protected her. Insisted that she get away from the area and go into hiding.

Fuller came to an abrupt stop, and Sammy slammed on his brakes, jumping out of the vehicle the moment he slipped the gear into Park. He ran past Officer Fuller, nearly falling on the slick, snowy road in his haste. The nose of Beth's BMW sloped downward, the front two tires completely depleted of air.

Her head and shoulders were slumped over the steering wheel, and her long brown hair hung down, veiling her face. In spite of all the chaotic sirens and lights, Beth wasn't moving. Sammy rapped his knuckles at the driver's-side windows before flinging open the door.

"Beth! What happened?"

No blood was visible on her body or in the car's interior, from where he stood. No apparent bullet wound. This was a good sign. His chest and lungs loosened a notch. Careful not to move her body in case of a neck or back injury, Sammy smoothed back her hair. Beth groaned and leaned back into the seat. Blood poured from a gash on her forehead. Her eyes flickered open, confusion clouding the gray irises. "Sammy?" she whispered, so softly he barely heard her.

"An ambulance is on the way. How badly are you hurt?"

She lifted an unsteady hand to her injured temple and frowned. "I… I'm not sure. Not too bad?"

The EMTs would be there in a moment. "Can you tell me what happened?"

"He shot at me."

"Who?"

"Don't know his name." She straightened and licked her lips. Color returned to her face as she apparently rose from the fog of unconsciousness. "I tried to call you."

"Right. I got your voice mail. Describe the man who harassed you. What exactly did he say?"

"Big giant of a guy with red hair who demanded I pay him fifty grand. He gave me a piece of paper with a phone number to call when I got the money together. When he left, I tried to follow him—"

"Damn it, Beth," he muttered.

"Coming through!" an EMT shouted by his elbow.

Their time was up. "Anything else you remember about the guy or the truck he drove?" he asked quickly.

"No."

Sammy nodded. "We're on it. If you think of something later, call me." He started to turn away, but Beth caught his arm. "Did you remember something?"

"I just wanted to say…" She offered a wan smile. "We should stop meeting like this."

Sammy stared at her dumbly before he realized Beth was making a joke.

Brad Pelling, an EMT he'd met many times, squeezed between him and Beth. "Got to do our job," he explained apologetically, feeling the pulse at Beth's neck.

"Of course." Sammy watched as Brad questioned Beth and continued taking her vital signs.

"She's fine." Charlotte moved to his side and searched his face, her eyes much too sharp and knowing. "Seems you are unusually focused on this particular victim."

"We've known each other for years. Her brother used to be a good friend." He gave a casual shrug but knew his partner wasn't fooled.

What was his deal when it came to Beth Wynngate? As he'd explained to Charlotte, she was merely an old friend's little sister. Nothing more or less.

But as Brad and another EMT pulled out a stretcher and laid Beth on it, he swallowed hard past a thick lump in his throat.

"Go with them and stay with Beth," Charlotte quietly urged. "I'll run what I can on the information she provided and ask around to see if there were any witnesses. If I come up with anything, I'll ring you."

He was torn between wanting to leap into the case and find who'd hurt Beth, and a desire to stay with her until she was released from the hospital.

"You know the hospital is unlikely to keep her overnight, even for a concussion," Charlotte said. "We need to consider how to protect her from another attack when they let her go."

That settled the matter. He forked over the cruiser keys. "Call me if you get any leads. After Beth is somewhere safe, I'll head to Atlanta and pay Lambert a surprise visit."

"Sounds like a plan. This situation with the Lambert family needs to be handled quickly before someone is seriously hurt or killed. Be careful."

"You, too." Bad enough he hadn't protected

Beth—he didn't need an injured partner on his conscience, as well. James Tedder, Charlotte's husband, was his best friend, and he'd be damned if James's wife and their future baby suffered because he'd overlooked a hidden danger.

Chapter Seven

Beth fought the effects of the prescription pain-killer and anti-inflammatory pills the hospital had administered. At least she'd talked them into giving her only a mild dosage. She'd need all her wits for the coming interview. Sammy didn't know it yet, but she was going to confront Dorsey Lambert. No way she'd miss the opportunity to get answers.

The rolling hills of North Georgia gave way to the crowded metro Atlanta area with its sky-scrapers and traffic. Lots of traffic. Gingerly, she touched the bandage by her temple.

"Your head starting to hurt?" Sammy asked.

"No." She shrugged and relented at his raised brows. "Well, maybe a little. I consider myself lucky not to have a concussion." She quickly rushed to change the subject. If she wanted to see Dorsey, she couldn't let Sammy harp on her injuries. He'd use it as an excuse to exclude her access. It'd been hard enough convincing him to let her go with him to Atlanta. "Does the traffic bother you?"

"It doesn't thrill me."

Sammy wasn't in the best of moods. En route, he'd contacted the Atlanta PD to provide backup while he questioned the suspect. They'd responded that there were no available officers and wouldn't be for several hours—if then. Sammy had told her that he'd almost turned around but decided the risk of her getting hurt again was greater than the danger of facing the man alone.

She covertly studied his profile. Sammy Armstrong was like a bad-luck charm that showed up at some of the worst moments in her life—the teenage arrest, the break-in at her house, and today's mess. But maybe it was good luck instead of bad, even the arrest. If he and his partner hadn't broken up the party when they did, the aftermath might have been even worse for her.

Sammy turned onto I-20, and a couple of miles later, they were driving through East Atlanta Village with its older homes, quirky shops and even an urban llama farm nestled less than a mile from the interstate mayhem. It was unlike the other parts of Atlanta Beth was used to. Their old family home, which Cynthia still occupied, was in Sandy Springs, which sported an old-money vibe with scenic mansions sprawled along single-lane roads. Aiden favored the affluent Buckhead area and lived in a high-rise condo near his law practice. Beth appreciated their different styles, but as for herself, she enjoyed the SoWa section in the South End of Boston, which served as a mecca of the arts.

Sammy pulled into the driveway of a modest ranch-style home with an old Plymouth Duster parked out front. He shut off the engine and then frowned when he caught her undoing her seat belt. "No way. You stay locked in here. It shouldn't take me long. Chances are he's not living here with his mother, anyway. Probably only listed her address to provide an answer on the Corrections release form."

"I'm not seeing her alone. I'm with an armed law enforcement officer. I couldn't possibly be any safer."

Lines creased on his forehead. "But—"

"No *buts*." Before he could answer, she hopped out of the car and shut the door. She offered him a breezy smile and sauntered toward the porch walkway.

Sammy exited the vehicle and let out a sigh that she guessed could be heard all the way down the street. "You let me do all the talking. I'll explain your presence as a recently hired detective. She'll assume you're in training. Agreed?"

"Of course," she assured him. *Unless I have a burning question for Lambert that you don't ask him yourself.* "Want me to stand at the back door in case he's home and tries to make a run for it?"

The look he threw her was so stern she instantly realized her mistake. "Just kidding," she offered. Quickly, she scooted up the porch steps in case he changed his mind. Sammy moved in front of her and rapped at the door.

A game show played on the TV until someone inside suddenly muted it. "Who's there?" called a raspy voice that could have been male or female.

"Elmore County Sheriff's Department."

Silence.

The peephole darkened briefly, and then the door flung open. A woman stood before them in a floral muumuu. Unkempt gray hair floated past her shoulders, and she sported the lip wrinkles associated with a long-term cigarette smoker. "You ain't got no jurisdiction in Fulton County," she pointed out in a gravelly voice. "What do you want?"

"Mrs. Rayna Lambert? We'd like a word with you about your son, Dorsey. You told Detective Tedder this morning that he lives with you at this address?"

"Like I told that woman, he ain't here," she offered unhelpfully. "He's at work down at the Coca Cola plant. Won't be home for hours."

"I'd like his cell phone number. I can meet him at the plant. Won't take but a few minutes of his time."

Rayna spat out a series of numbers that Sammy punched in his own phone. Beth peered past the woman's bulky frame and into the den, which was surprisingly well furnished and neat. Mrs. Lambert took more care with her housekeeping than she did her personal appearance. From the den, she had a view of the kitchen and a hallway that led to more rooms and a back door. A flash of red hair poked from one of the hallway rooms. The man had a gaunt, pale face with eyes focused on where they stood on the porch. He had the intent furtiveness of a hunted animal assessing danger. He caught her stare, and his eyes widened. Before she could alert Sammy, the man bolted from the room and sprinted to the back door.

"Hey, he's here!" she said, tugging on Sammy's jacket. "He's making a run for the back!"

"Halt," he called out, trying to push past Rayna Lambert's hulking frame. "We just have a few questions."

"Guess he don't want to talk to you," she said without a trace of humor in her flat voice.

Sammy flew down the steps. "Get in the car," he ordered.

Like hell. Beth waited until he'd sped past the corner of the house before she ran after him.

Magnolia trees haphazardly dotted the large backyard, but enough snow lay on the ground to show Lambert's footprints leading straight to the neighbor's abutting property. Lambert was thin and lithe and had the adrenaline rush of the hunted as he scaled the privacy fence and disappeared from her sight. Sammy was close behind, and he also quickly climbed over.

Unlike Aiden, she'd never been the athletic type, preferring the solitary pursuit of painting while he went to ball practice. Scaling a six-foot fence was not in her wheelhouse, especially after being banged up in the car. Instead, she sped to the side of the property, arriving in time to watch as Sammy pursued Lambert down the tree-lined street and then around the bend in the road.

Should she call 911? She tapped the cell phone in her back pocket but decided Sammy might not appreciate her interference. It might be best to let him either apprehend Dorsey on his own or make arrangements to return later with a police officer. But retreat to the cruiser?

Beth slowly turned around, facing Rayna, who stood rooted on the back porch, hands crossed over her chest, watching the drama with a stone-faced expression.

Dorsey might have given them the slip, but his mother hadn't. She slowly walked toward her, as though Rayna were a wild animal who'd balk at the slightest provocation and retreat into her lair. But the Lambert matriarch was made of sterner stuff than that. She eyed Beth dead-on and never flinched a muscle, even though her son was running from the law, even though she was clad only in a thin housedress in the frigid cold—cold for Atlanta, that was—and even though a stranger approached.

Beth stopped at the edge of the back porch, staring into the woman's implacable face. "Why?" she asked simply.

Rayna pulled a pack of cigarettes and a lighter from the pocket of her dress, expertly cupped her hands over her mouth to shield the flame from the wind, and lit up. She drew heavily and then exhaled a noxious cloud of gray smoke. "Why what?" she asked abruptly.

"Why is your son out to get me?"

"First of all, I don't even know who the hell you are."

"Beth Wynngate."

"Ah." The pale eyes flickered. "You must be

related to Judge Edward Wynngate." She spat out the name as though she'd accidentally swallowed a morsel of something putrid.

Beth squared her shoulders, unashamed to claim the familial connection. "His daughter."

Rayna cast disapproving eyes over her from head to toe, and Beth was conscious of how she must appear to the older woman—a tasteful Berber knitted cap with matching scarf, diamond studs discreetly gleaming on her earlobes, a wool coat of the finest quality, tailored trousers and designer boots. And there was also the little matter of the bandage over her right temple.

"Go on," Rayna urged. "What's Dorsey done got himself into?"

"I've been threatened. Several times." She touched the bandage. "Most recently this morning. Your son seems to hold some kind of grudge against my father—who died seven months ago, by the way."

If she'd expected sympathy, she'd have been disappointed. Rayna's features didn't soften for an instant.

"Anyway, a man confronted me this morning, saying I needed to fork over fifty thousand dollars to make all this go away."

"But it weren't Dorsey."

"No. But it has to be someone he sent, probably a member of the family, judging by the red hair."

"Sounds like a pretty flimsy connection to me."

She didn't want to give away any specific information to this woman, so she merely stated the obvious. "Oh yeah? Then why'd your son run from us?"

"He's an ex-convict. Why wouldn't his first instinct be to run from the cops? He never wants to be behind bars again." She drew on the cigarette. "I don't want that for him, either."

"Then work with us. If Dorsey isn't behind this, he can clear his name."

"Like you'd believe anything he'd say."

"Can you just get him to leave me alone?" she asked, burying her pride. "I haven't done anything to him. Whatever grudge he had with my father, that's in the past. The man's dead, and his sentencing was always fair and within the bounds of the law. This vendetta is ridiculous."

"Poor little rich girl. Daddy's dead, and here you stand, looking like a million bucks. Must have inherited a nice bundle."

Beth said nothing. What was the point in denial?

Rayna tilted her head back and blew out a series of spiral smoke rings. "I'll tell you this much," she said at last. "Dorsey may be a lot of things. Bad things. But he ain't gonna rough up no woman. And he certainly ain't a killer."

Delusional mother. "Maybe you don't know him as well as you think you do. And what about the rest of the family?"

Rayna tossed the cigarette in the snow, snuffing it out. "I'll speak to him."

"Thank you." A modicum of relief swept through her. Even if Sammy couldn't catch up to Dorsey, perhaps some good had come out of this trip.

"I ain't doin' it for you, missy." Rayna started to turn away. "Now get the hell off my property."

What are you going to do if I refuse, call the cops? But of course, Beth didn't say it aloud. No point in antagonizing the woman and calling her out over an idle threat. Rayna retreated inside, and the door slammed shut.

Beth hunched forward, bracing against a chilly gust of wind. Where was Sammy? Was he okay? Dorsey's small build wouldn't match up well with Sammy's fit, muscular body, but a cornered rat might prove dangerous. If she had the cruiser keys, she could search the neighborhood. She was just lucky he'd left it unlocked for her.

She looked over her shoulder, but there was

no sign of either man. Might as well wait in the warm car rather than stand out here in the cold, her very presence ticking off Rayna Lambert, a possible ally. And even if she didn't want to admit it to Sammy, her head and back ached from the wreck. She'd been lucky the guardrails had held and that her car hadn't crashed down the mountain. Just imagining being trapped inside the twisted metal heap as it flipped and landed in the hollow below made her knees weak.

Once in the cruiser, Beth leaned back in the seat and closed her eyes, willing herself to relax and have faith that Sammy knew what he was doing and was in no danger. They'd caught Dorsey unawares, so it was unlikely he had a weapon on him as he'd raced from the house. Actually, he'd been wearing a T-shirt and long johns, and he'd been barefoot. A distinct disadvantage against Sammy. She hoped that helped make up for Sammy's lack of knowledge about the layout of the neighborhood, but she pictured Dorsey slunk below the foundation of someone's house, curled into a tight ball like a stray animal hiding.

The car door suddenly slung open, and she jumped in her seat. Her heart jackhammered against her ribs until she saw it was Sammy.

Alone.

"He got away, huh?" she asked. "Figures. He's like a pesky rodent scurrying out of trouble."

"I'd say more than pesky," he answered, pointing at her injury.

Sammy started the car, and they rolled away. A slight lift of the curtain at the front of the house told Beth that Dorsey's mother had been keeping a close watch. Her son would slither back home soon enough.

"Are you going to contact the Atlanta PD again and update them?"

"Already did." His jaw was tight and his hands white-knuckled as they gripped the steering wheel. "I knew I should have waited until they had an officer available."

"You couldn't have known if Dorsey would even be home tonight," she pointed out. "Are we going to drive around the neighborhood and see if he's around?"

"We can. The local cops agreed to put out a BOLO. Maybe they'll capture him."

He circled around the block and then widened the search to another neighborhood in the direction Dorsey had run.

"Could be he's got friends or relatives close by that've already taken him in. But the good news is that Rayna Lambert agreed to see if she could talk some sense into her son."

Sammy snorted. "Don't count on that happening. Apple doesn't usually fall far from the tree."

Let him be cynical. Beth believed Rayna would try. After all, she was his mother, and it was obvious that if Dorsey didn't stop pursuing her, this wouldn't end well for him. "Time will tell," she said in a you'll-see tone.

"This is pointless," Sammy said at last, running a hand through his dark hair. "Now to figure out what to do with you."

"What do you mean?"

"You're obviously not safe in Blood Mountain. While we're in Atlanta, maybe you should pay your stepmother a visit. Surely you can stay with her until Lambert is apprehended."

The too-casual way Sammy threw out the suggestion didn't fool her. She had the sneaking suspicion this had been his intent all along in coming to Atlanta—to dump her off on Cynthia. Her stepmother would hate that even more than she would.

"No way. I'll take my chances back home."

"Home? Meaning…you're going back to Boston?"

"Blood Mountain." Strange that she considered it home rather than her dad's old house in Sandy Springs or her apartment in Boston.

He frowned. "Then stay with Aiden."

"He's still out of town."

Sammy pulled onto the interstate, his fingers tapping out a beat against the dashboard. "There has to be a safe place for you somewhere." He cleared his throat, as if uncomfortable with what he was about to say. "Would you consider staying with me? I have a guest room." His voice was no-nonsense, but she detected a note of tension in it, as if afraid of her answer.

"Nope. That's not happening. I can't imagine your boss would cotton to that idea, either."

"Harlan's a friend. Speaking of which, Charlotte mentioned you could stay with Lilah, if being with me bothers you so much."

"Lilah's busy. I wouldn't feel right imposing. Not when her baby's due any moment."

"Stubborn," he mumbled, shifting in his seat.

"I heard that." She wasn't offended, though, especially considering that it was the truth. She'd lived too long in places where she wasn't truly wanted. Once she'd left high school, she'd sworn she'd never again be a millstone around another person's neck.

"There's always Boston." Her heart wasn't in the suggestion, though, since it had proven unsafe once before. But it would put distance between her and the Lamberts.

"That's no good. You were followed up there."

"True. But I think Rayna can put a stop to Dorsey's stalking."

"Don't kid yourself on that score." He shot her a hooded glance. "Is the thought of staying with me so disagreeable? Are you worried about what people will say?"

"It's not that."

"Then what is it?"

"I won't put anyone else in danger again."

"I can take care of myself while I protect you. For crying out loud, Beth. I'm a cop."

"Out of the question," she insisted.

Sammy shook his head and mouthed the word *stubborn*.

She was refusing for his own good, even if he couldn't see it. His offer was tempting. But no matter how easily Sammy shrugged off the impropriety, it wouldn't look good for him professionally to have her, a targeted victim, living in his home. So the problem remained. Where could she stay, besides possibly a string of impersonal hotels, where no Lambert would find her? Someplace where her presence wouldn't be a danger to her host?

A fully formed image blasted into her mind—a small but comfortable cabin near Lavender Mountain's peak. Her dad's former hunting cabin was so isolated that she doubted anyone else even knew of its existence.

If she couldn't hide out there in the wilds, then no place was safe.

Chapter Eight

"I don't like it," Sammy said as he finally spotted the tiny lodge almost hidden from sight. Although the oak trees and shrubs were bare, the wooden structure melded seamlessly behind a copse of evergreen pines, and snow covered its roof.

"You haven't even been inside yet. Give it a chance," Beth said.

His Jeep jostled as he hit a pothole. The dirt road had become so overgrown from a long period of no travelers that tree branches arching from each side of the embankment met in the middle to form a gnarled, brown tunnel. Limbs scratched the sides of his vehicle; the metal frame rubbing dead wood sounded like a knife scraping against a plate. His forearms momentarily goose-bumped at the high-octave screech.

"Jeep's going to need a paint job before this is over," he grumbled.

She grinned back at him. "Jeeps are made for off-road use. The scratches will give it character."

He couldn't help returning the grin. With every mile they'd put between them and Atlanta, Beth had visibly relaxed. He didn't share her confidence that the danger was past, but he took heart that she seemed to have forgiven him for daring to question her father's integrity. Unless absolutely necessary, he wouldn't tread again in that emotional quagmire.

He pulled the vehicle as close as possible to the cabin, but they still had to trudge a good twenty yards with all the supplies they'd picked up in town after he'd swapped out the cruiser for his own vehicle. Quickly, they hauled their stash inside, hoping to get everything unloaded and a fire started before the sun set. Already the shadows lengthened, birds flocked noisily to find their night's resting place, and the air grew chillier. Night fell quickly in the mountains, and with the darkness came an almost unsettling quiet.

Sammy paused in his work, a pile of firewood in his arms, and surveyed the land. How many years had it been since he and Harlan and James had spent a weekend hunting? Too many. His friends were busy with their own families now, and the realization briefly pinched his heart. *It's understandable. They've moved on.* Once their children were older, they'd probably be able to get away for an occasional all-guy trip. As for himself, the whole marriage-and-kiddos thing held no appeal. He'd seen how much a bad marriage could devastate a man. His dad had been proof of that.

A loud clatter erupted from the cabin, and his heart hammered. He dropped the pile of wood and raced inside. Had the cabin been booby-trapped? A string tied to a shotgun trigger or trip wires set to an explosive? The Lambert men were rugged mountain folks with little regard for the law and notorious for holding grudges. If they knew of the cabin and had gotten there first...

Beth stood in the kitchen, arms akimbo, staring at the dozens of food cans rolling around the rough pine floor. She held up a brown sack with a torn bottom by way of explanation.

He huffed out a breath of relief, almost laughing at his imagination.

"Didn't mean to scare you," she said.

"Are you sure no one outside of your family knows about this place?"

"How many times do I have to assure you? I'm positive no one else has seen this place, not even hikers or hunters. It's isolated, yes, but that's an advantage. No one knows about it. It's private property. I doubt Cynthia and Aiden even come here. Aiden only bothered with it when he wanted to throw parties far away from parental eyes."

Sammy bent down and helped her pick up the strewn cans. "Still can't believe Judge Wynngate liked to hunt. Didn't picture him as an outdoors kind of guy."

"Dad grew up in the North Carolina mountains. That's why he bought the house at Falling Rock and then built this cabin as his own private retreat. His job dictated he live in a big city, but he enjoyed time in nature."

He caught the wistful note in her voice. "I also had the impression that you and your father weren't all that close."

"Not since I was a little girl," she admitted. "When Mom died of cancer, a part of my dad seemed to wither away, even after he married Cynthia a few years later. And once I became a teenager…well, things changed between us."

Sammy was well aware of the wedge her arrest had driven between Beth and her family—an arrest he was partially responsible for making. "I remember your mom. Nice lady."

Beth's gray eyes brightened. "You do?"

"Yep. I do."

A charged silence fell between them, and he was intensely aware of the closeness of her body, the soft floral scent that was always a part of Beth. With just the two of them alone inside the cozy cabin, it seemed they were isolated from the rest of the world.

He stepped backward, breaking the spell. Protecting Beth was his job, and he'd better remember that fact. "I'll get the rest of the stuff in before it gets too dark."

"Right," she quickly agreed, her cheeks flushed pink. "Lots to do before I get settled in."

"Before *we* get settled in," he corrected.

"I already told you, I'm fine out here. Perfectly safe. No need—"

"I'm staying," he insisted. "At least for tonight."

Actually, he planned to stay with her until he got word that the Atlanta PD had Lambert in custody. But he'd fight that battle with Beth later. One day at a time. And who knew? By tomorrow, Dorsey Lambert indeed might be locked away.

Outside, Sammy inhaled the bracing winter air. *This is business only*, he reminded himself. *Get a grip.* He brought in the rest of the boxes from the Jeep. Amazing how much stuff you needed to bring along, even for a short visit. Once all was unloaded, he set to work building a fire. It didn't take long for the small interior to be filled with its warmth and the pleasant scent of burning oak.

"Your gourmet meal awaits," Beth said, carrying their take-out food on a tray into the living area. She'd placed the Mexican fast-food dishes on plates and filled two glasses with soda. They sat across from one another as they ate, Beth on a chair she'd pulled over to the coffee table, while he sprawled on the leather sofa. He dipped a tortilla chip into the salsa bowl and pointed at the canvas frame she'd set in the corner of the room. A sheet draped the front. "What are you working on?"

"A snowscape of Blood Mountain."

"May I see?"

Color rose on her cheeks. "It's not finished yet. Since there's no television up here, I figured I'd pass the time painting. Maybe start a few new ones."

She didn't feel comfortable sharing her work with him. "I suppose most artists don't like showing their works in progress. I can respect that. As someone who has zippo artistic talent, I have to say that I admire seeing it in others," he said.

The blue specks in her dove-gray eyes shimmered as she silently regarded him. "You have an interest in the arts?"

"Who doesn't?" he countered with a shrug.

"I may not have access to local museums like you do in Boston, but I can still appreciate beauty. I just get mine from a different source. Like walking through the woods or driving around mountain roads with panoramic views of Appalachia."

"Touché," she said, lifting her glass of soda in a mock toast and taking a swallow. "I wish my family had half as much appreciation for art as you do. They see my painting as dabbling. A hobby. And the art classes I teach middle graders? It's not a distinguished enough career for their respect. They act embarrassed when their friends ask what I do in Boston."

Sammy wasn't surprised. Cynthia Wynngate appeared the sort to only care about social prestige, and Aiden had adopted his mother's attitude over the years. He and Aiden had drifted apart soon after Aiden started college. Sammy heard his former friend spent summers hanging out in the city with new buddies, tossing around money without limits. On the few occasions Sammy had run into Aiden, there had been a subtle change in the way Aiden treated him. Without sports, they'd discovered they had no common interests, and even short conversations became awkward.

"I'm sorry," he said. "I hope their attitude doesn't upset you. It's their problem, not yours."

A genuine smile lit her face. "It doesn't bother me. Not much, anyway. Besides, I only see them once or twice a year. No big deal."

He hoped that was true.

She gestured at the canvas frame. "You can look, if you'd like."

"You're sure?"

"Yes. Just don't expect Van Gogh or something."

He stood and crossed the room, but she remained seated. Carefully, he lifted the sheet and stared at the painting. A plumage of white, yellow, pink and coral clouds drifted over the mountains dotted green with pine and espresso-colored oak trees, their branches glinting with ice. Old Man Brooks's abandoned red barn adorned the right corner of the canvas. The wide swath of snow blanketing the ground reflected the sky's multicolored palette.

Sammy stared at it for long moments before speaking. He felt like he could step into that scene of crisp pastoral elegance. "It's beautiful," he said simply, then turned to look her in the eyes.

"You mean it?" She rose and sauntered toward him. "It still needs a few finishing touches."

"I mean it."

"Thanks, Sammy." Her breathy voice was

close by his side, and he swallowed hard. He scanned a couple more paintings, all in various stages of completion, all alive with pastel washes of color. He knew little of art, but he recognized talent when he saw it. Beth had it. Looking at her work was unexpectedly intimate, as though by viewing her art, he glimpsed something of her soul and how she perceived the beauty in the world. Slowly, he faced her.

Firelight flickered golden on her face, neck and arms. Thin strands of cinnamon highlights streaked her sleek sable hair, and Beth's understated beauty made his breath hitch. As it had been earlier in the kitchen, everything seemed to still. There was only the two of them, alone, with the fireplace crackling in the background. His gaze drifted to her lips. Just one taste. What was the harm? Her mouth parted, and she almost imperceptibly leaned into him. This was it. This was the moment. Sammy bowed his head and pressed his lips to hers. They were as warm and intoxicating as he'd imagined.

He lost himself in the softness of her lips. This was where he was always meant to be. As though the kiss had been inevitable from the moment he saw her again, looking shaken by the threatening letter but determined to get to the bottom of the matter.

Aiden's little sister all grown up.

A barred owl screeched nearby, invading his senses, which had grown thick and heavy with passion. He clasped his hands under her forearms and pulled away. He was supposed to be there to protect Beth, not make love to her. "This isn't a good idea."

Beth stared at him wide-eyed, one hand drifting up to touch her lips. Confusion, then hurt, and at last, resignation flashed across her face. "You're probably right."

Part of him wished she'd protested, but a saner inner voice assured him he'd done the right thing. They returned to dinner and went to bed early, Beth retiring to the one bedroom on the other side of the kitchen while he lay on the sofa under a woolen blanket. For hours he stared into the fireplace as the flames crackled, and then the logs dwindled to blazing orange embers. Had pulling away from Beth been a mistake? The longer he lay awake, the less confident he became of his decision. There were so many reasons not to get involved with her—it would be unprofessional; she lived hundreds of miles away; she resented him for arresting her years ago; and the Wynngates were in a different social league. The distance between them and the reasons to keep it that way seemed impenetrable.

Yet he couldn't deny that their kiss had shaken him to his core.

DAWN FILTERED THROUGH the small window of the cabin. Beth huddled deeper beneath the quilt, reluctant to leave the lazy warmth of the featherbed. And getting up meant facing Sammy, who'd delivered a mind-blowing kiss only to reject her moments later.

But what a kiss.

Somehow she'd have to pretend it had never happened and just get on with the day. Surely he didn't plan to hang around too long? She'd have to convince him there was no danger so far into the woods. She'd be careful to keep the doors locked, her shotgun loaded and at the ready. After all, this was her cabin, and she got to decide who had permission to come and go. Being alone was what she needed. Without the distraction of television and the internet, she'd absorb herself with painting, and when she tired of that, she'd curl up in bed with a good book. Plan made, she pulled on jeans and a sweatshirt and headed to the kitchen.

Sammy was already up. He sat on the edge of the sofa, drinking his usual morning drink of soda, and raised his head at her approach. His jaw had an unshaven shadow that looked sexy as hell.

"Good morning," she called out airily. "I'm up. You should head on back to work now."

"I'm not leaving."

"Doesn't your partner need you?"

"Not as much as you do."

"Don't be ridiculous. I'll lock the door behind you. Any sign of trouble, I'll call 911." She nodded at the shotgun above the fireplace. "And don't forget I have a weapon." Beth turned her back on him and rummaged through the cooler for an orange juice pack. "Did you ever call Cynthia about the break-in?"

"Yep. And got her permission to have a tech guy search your dad's computer." He took a seat at the kitchen table and eyed her curiously. "Your stepmother didn't tell you?"

"She called early yesterday morning, but I was talking to Lilah at the time. The right moment to call her back just didn't happen. Too much going on."

Understatement of the year. Luckily, Sammy didn't bother pointing out that now was as good a time as any. She'd call Cynthia back later today, once she was alone and not so frazzled. Beth sat across from Sammy at the table, then picked up a small metal cylinder that hadn't been there last night. "What's this?"

"Pepper spray. Keep it clipped on a belt or a

loop on your jeans. It's police-strength and has a range of ten feet."

She eyed it warily. "I'm afraid I'll hurt myself more than the criminal I'm aiming at. How's it work?"

"It's easy. I'll show you."

Sammy demonstrated how to rotate the trigger to the fire position.

"What if I accidently spray myself?"

"You won't."

"Okay. If it makes you feel better." She looped the canister onto her jeans, privately resolving to take it off the moment he finally left.

"Have you ever shot a pistol?"

"No, but Dad taught me to use the shotgun."

"I can teach you—"

"No, thanks. I'm good."

"Then I insist you at least let me teach you a few self-defense moves."

She started to object, then closed her mouth, remembering the tall stranger from yesterday looming over her. "Not a bad idea."

"How sore is your back?"

"Surprisingly good. No headache, either."

"Great." He slammed both hands on the table. "Grab your jacket, and let's get to work."

"Can't we do it in the den?"

"Not enough space."

"Fine," she muttered, grabbing her designer jacket.

Sammy paused in the doorway and cocked his head toward the fireplace mantel, where the shotgun hung. "That thing loaded?"

"Yes."

"I'll test it and make sure it's in running order. Bring it along with that box of extra shells on the sofa."

Beth picked up the items and followed him out the door. How long could it take? Fifteen, maybe twenty minutes tops, and then she'd have the cabin to herself.

They trudged through the snow a good distance to get to a clearing wide enough to test the shotgun. "This'll do," he said at last.

She handed him the gun, and he checked the barrel. Satisfied, he lifted it to his shoulder and shot off a round. Even though she expected it, the blast in the forest silence made her jump. It'd been over a decade since she'd come out here with Dad and shot cans off a fallen tree log for target practice. Back before their falling-out over the party.

"Your turn."

She took the shotgun, steeled her legs in anticipation of the kickback and fired off a round. It felt good. No one would find her out here in the boonies, but if worse came to worst, she wouldn't hesitate to protect herself. She raised the gun in one hand. "Who needs self-defense moves when you've got this?"

"Can't carry it with you everywhere, every moment."

Beth carefully set the shotgun against a tree, resigned to another lesson. "Show me what I need to learn."

Sammy shrugged out of his jacket and tossed it on the ground. "First demonstration. Say your attacker approaches you from the front and grabs your arm." He clamped his hand down on her right forearm and regarded her sternly. "How would you try to escape this hold?"

"Kick you in the nuts?" she guessed.

"Wrong. He'd see it coming and block it." Sammy placed her left fist on his hand that was clutching her arm. "Now point your left elbow up, and then slice down with every muscle in your core."

She tried, but Sammy held fast.

"Give it all you've got," he urged. "Muscle and weight."

It took several attempts, but to her surprise, the move worked to free her from Sammy's grip.

"Good job. Now let's try a different scenario. Let's say someone grabs you from behind and places his arms around your waist."

Sammy moved behind her and held her tight in his arms. His hard body pressed against her back, and heat flared through her. The memory of last night's kiss fueled her awareness of him. If she turned her head an inch to one side, her lips would land on his chin, and then his mouth would seek hers, and—

His arms clenched tighter around her abs and squeezed. "Pay attention," he said, his voice harsh and deep in her ears.

The warm rush of his breath sent shivers down to her core. How could she possibly concentrate when her mind was thick with the possibilities of the two of them kissing? With great effort, she shook off the images playing in her head. "I'm listening," she said. "What do I do next?"

"Grab my arms and then pull yourself in."

"Like this?" she asked, holding tight to his arms.

"That's it. Now swing your hips to one side and make a fist."

Surprisingly, she felt his hold give way, and she held up her fist. "Now what?"

"If this was an attacker, you'd strike his groin with that fist. Hard as you can."

"That should buy me a few seconds," she remarked dryly.

"Use that time to run. If you're out in public,

scream as loudly as you can." He frowned. "Next time I'm at the office, I'll get you a whistle."

Beth stepped away from him, glad to put a little distance between them. "Thanks. I'll keep these moves in mind."

He looked at her in surprise. "We're not nearly through yet."

"We aren't?"

"I've got a couple more moves to show you, and then you're going to practice until your reactions become automatic. Otherwise, you won't remember any of this if an attacker comes at you with no warning."

Sweat trickled down her neck and chest, despite the cold air and snow. Beth shrugged out of her coat as Sammy had done earlier. Over and over, they rehearsed her reactions for every eventuality, whether she was attacked from the front or behind.

"Remember the key vulnerable areas—eyes, nose, throat and groin," he kept reminding her. "Use your head and stay aware of your surroundings. If an attacker aims a gun at you, then run away in a zigzag pattern while seeking shelter."

Forty-five minutes later, Beth's body dripped head to toe with sweat, and she was panting. But she was prepared. "I'm feeling pretty badass," she said with a cocky grin.

Sammy didn't return the smile, still intent on drilling home his message. He made a sudden lunge for her, and she raised her fists by her face, ready to fight. Again and again Sammy came at her, and she fended him off. At last he broke away and gave an approving nod. "I think you've got it. One last thing. If you have no choice but to fight back, commit to it and never hesitate to hit as hard as you can." His eyes darkened. "If you do get overpowered, fake compliance, and then strike again or run at the first opportunity."

"Got it," she said. Beth had never felt more competent. If someone did try to take her by force, she'd at least put up a good fight.

Chapter Nine

"So how come you never got married?"

Sammy nearly choked on the vegetable soup they ate for dinner in front of the fireplace.

A flash of worry flickered in Beth's eyes. "Or are you?"

"Wh-what?" he stammered, clearing his throat. His eyes watered, and he hastily swallowed iced tea.

"You okay there?" Beth placed her hand between his shoulder blades and patted.

"What in the world brought on that question?"

She shrugged. "Why not? I mean, we're stuck out here together. Nothing else to do but talk."

He quirked a brow at her. He could think of plenty of things to do besides talking. If she noticed his amusement, she pretended otherwise.

"Well, are you?" she prodded.

"I'm not married, although I was engaged once." He hadn't thought of Emily in years.

"How long ago? What happened?"

"Years ago."

Beth's gray eyes remained pinned on him.

"She dumped me for another guy."

Her mouth rounded in an O of surprise and sympathy flooded her face. "That's horrible. I'm so sorry that—"

Sammy held up a hand. "It was my fault. She kept pressuring me to set a date and I wasn't ready. Frankly, getting engaged had been a mistake from the beginning. It was a decision I later regretted."

"Why? Did you fall out of love? Realize she wasn't the right woman for you?"

More like cold feet. Actually, that had been more than half of the problem. Sammy moved his bowl to the side and faced Beth where she sat opposite him. They were both cross-legged on the floor, casually dining in front of the fireplace—the only warm spot in the cabin. He could give a short nod to her questions, because Beth was partly right, but he wanted honesty between them.

"The idea of tying myself down forever to one woman and raising kids scared the hell out of me," he admitted. "Judging by my parents' marriage, it's a miserable way to live. Guess you've heard stories about my dad. It's a small town."

Her forehead creased, and she bit her lip. "You're almost a decade older than me so it's not like we ran in the same circles. But it seems like I did overhear that he had a drinking problem."

"Stone-cold alcoholic." Sammy drew a deep breath and decided to rip the bandage off as it were. "Mom ran off with my high school math teacher when I was a junior. Even though the marriage had never been great, it broke Dad. He started drinking heavily."

Sammy kept his face averted, not wanting to see the sympathy in Beth's eyes. He believed in letting the past stay buried and rarely mentioned either of his parents.

"That must have been horrible for you as a teenager. I had no idea. You always seemed so happy and cheerful when I saw you with Aiden."

All an act. Sports had been a lifesaver in his teenage years. While Dad spent most of his free time at local bars, playing ball had given him an activity to focus on instead of sitting alone in a dark and cold house waiting for parents who'd both deserted him—in mind if not in body.

"It wasn't that big of a deal," he lied.

Beth's hands closed over his fists. He hadn't even realized he'd clenched his hands into hard knots, or that his body was wound up tight as a swollen tick. Not until the warm softness of Beth's fingers caressed his knuckles, bathing him with light.

"Of course it was a big deal," she murmured. She squeezed his hands and let go. "Do you regret letting her get away?"

"Who?" he asked, confused at the question.

"Your ex-fiancée."

"Emily?" He chuckled. "Not at all. I run into her from time to time. She's happily married with two boys. I'm glad for her. It's what she always wanted. What about you?" Turnabout was fair play.

"Me?"

"Why aren't you married?" That was the real mystery. A woman with her looks, brains and talent must have been hotly pursued.

"Guess the right guy hasn't come along yet. I've had a few close relationships but…" Her voice trailed off.

"I call bullshit."

Instead of taking offense, Beth laughed. "You might say I fundamentally distrust most people. That doesn't make for strong, lasting relationships."

"You trusted Rayna Lambert yesterday."

"Maybe I just wanted to believe there was an easy way out of this mess. That a mom can appeal to her son's basic decency and set everything right."

"That outcome's highly doubtful."

"True."

She turned her head toward the hearth and he watched the play of fire glow on her elegant features. "You seem to trust me," he ventured.

"Also true."

Perhaps she'd had no choice but to do so. "You can, you know," he said gently. "Trust me, that is. I won't let anyone hurt you."

"You can't make a promise like that."

"I just did."

She fixed her attention on him again. "This—" she swept the room with her hand "—is only a brief respite, not a fun getaway in the woods, much as I try to pretend that it is."

"There's plenty going on behind the scenes while we hide out. Charlotte's working on the case, and the Atlanta PD will eventually pick Lambert up now that he's on their radar. Until Lambert's accounted for, this is our best option." He cocked his head to the side and studied Beth. "Is it so bad being stuck with me?"

"Of course not. Only it feels like my entire life's on hold. It's frustrating. I came down to visit friends and family and instead I'm burrowed underground like a mole."

"Not for long." At least, he hoped that was the case. This morning, Charlotte had informed him that Judge Wynngate's computer hard drive was sent to a tech specialist in Atlanta, but that she'd been unable to place a priority on the task. A stalking case in Appalachia didn't rank high in their opinion. To be fair, they had murders and kidnapping cases that rightly took precedent. There was never enough manpower to investigate every potential crime risk.

"Some visit," she mumbled.

Visit. Meaning she'd be leaving soon. He'd managed to keep pushing that bit of reality from his mind. Getting too close to Beth would be a mistake.

So why did his arms reach for her, draw her close into an embrace? He rested his head on the top of her scalp, inhaling the clean scent of shampoo. Her hair was silky and warm against his cheek. She wiggled closer into him. Side by side they watched the flames in the fireplace leap and play in the darkness. Night came early in the mountain woods and it lay thick around them. With no neighbors and no electricity, the only light outside came from moonbeams reflecting on the pristine snowy ground.

He rained down kisses, starting at the top of

her scalp, and then trailing the side of her face. Beth turned into him, her lips seeking his own. His tongue sought hers and she moaned softly as her arms wrapped behind his neck, urging him closer—deeper.

She could be gone tomorrow. Sammy tamped down the thought as her fingers traced the nape of his neck and then stroked his hair. *This can never last.* Damn that incessant, rational voice in his brain that fired off warning missiles.

Beth climbed into his lap and straddled him, never breaking their kiss. His pulse skyrocketed, and a fever of need coursed through his body. *She'll only leave you.*

That got his attention. The thought triggered his dad's often-repeated words about how women always left you high and dry and to never trust them.

Sammy broke off the kiss, cupping Beth's chin in his hands. Her eyes were graphite-dark and clouded with passion and her lips were swollen and moist. How could he possibly say *no* to this magic between them?

He couldn't.

And he was experienced enough to know this was more than a physical reaction. Blended with the raw passion was tenderness and awe. His heart was in so much trouble.

Abruptly, Beth stood and then pulled her

sweater and T-shirt over her head. Her long, dark hair wildly tumbled around her pale shoulders. His throat went dry as she locked her gaze with his and unhooked her bra. The sight of her semi-naked body took his breath away. Sammy couldn't even speak. Instead, he held out his hand. Beth took it and she kneeled in front of him. Impatiently he pulled loose and stripped out of his T-shirt and then his jeans. Her eyes devoured him as he shed everything and stood before her, his need evident.

And then he was beside her, lying on the soft rug, their bodies pressed against each other. Who cared about tomorrow when tonight was so entrancing? For now there was only the heat of the fire on their nude bodies, the heat of bare skin brushing against bare skin, and the heat of need bubbling inside him like a fiery cauldron.

Much, much later, Sammy drifted in the twilight between sleep and wakefulness as Beth lay sound asleep beside him. He tucked the quilt she'd brought from the bedroom around her shoulders and smiled as she sighed and snuggled closer into the warmth of his body. A peaceful, contented drowsiness lazed through him.

Right now, holding Beth after a night of lovemaking had to be a top ten moment in his life. Scratch that, top five at least. Maybe even the best moment he'd ever experienced… Quickly, Sammy eradicated the thought. The sexual afterglow had clouded his perspective. There was no need to rank or analyze what he was feeling. *Just enjoy this time while it lasts.* Determined to follow his own advice, Sammy yawned and succumbed to the lethargy.

Through the fog of sleep, a slight noise pricked his awareness. Sammy mentally swatted at it, annoyed at the disruption, and drifted back into a doze. A slight flicker of light disturbed the inky darkness behind his eyelids. A slight crackling erupted from the silence, probably the dying flames consuming the last of the oak. Come morning, he'd add more wood to the fire.

Crunch.

Sammy's eyes popped open, alertness splashing over him like icy water. His body tensed, ready to spring into action. A quick glance assured him Beth still slept undisturbed by his side. He waited, as still as a cat ready to pounce.

Crunch, crunch and then *crunch, crunch.* The sound of advancing footsteps muffled in the snow.

Someone had found them.

This was bad. There'd been no noise or oncoming headlights from a car. No phone communication from the outside world warning of an emergency visit. It had to be Lambert or one of his men. Sammy eased the blanket off while his eyes searched the dark room. The fireplace embers provided just enough light to locate his pistol set on the mantel. Slowly, he rose and grabbed it, the cold metal gripped in his palm reassuring. Beth turned restlessly, pulling the quilt up until it almost covered her face.

He pondered the wisdom of waking her. The advantage would be that she'd be his backup, armed with a shotgun. The disadvantage would be that in waking Beth, he'd startle her, and she'd make a noise, alerting whoever was out there that they were awake and onto them. Swiftly, he decided to rouse her. He couldn't very well leave her alone and vulnerable while he searched out the danger.

Noiselessly, he kneeled and placed a hand on her shoulder. No response. He gave her shoulder a little shake. Her eyes flew open in alarm, then softened when she focused on him. Keeping his gun in his right hand, Sammy lifted the index finger of his opposite hand and pressed it against his puckered lips.

Hush.

Her eyes widened with fear, but she nodded understanding. He pointed at his gun and then to the fireplace. *Get your shotgun.* Nimbly, she tossed aside the quilt and rose. They both had on sweats they'd donned before falling asleep in the chilly cabin. He saw her scoop up her cell phone and shove it into a pocket as she went to the mantel. When she held the shotgun, he raised a palm toward her. *Stay here.*

Beth violently shook her head *no.* He glared at her and she returned his gaze with equal determination. Seemed he had a backup after all.

Sammy leaned into her and whispered in her ear. "Someone's out there. I'm going outside."

Beth nodded and whispered, "Let's go."

"Stay behind me."

He walked to the door and disengaged the lock. A barely audible click sounded before he slid the metal bolts to the side. Fighting an instinct to fling open the door and run wildly into the dark, Sammy turned the knob, conscious of Beth's soft breathing behind him and the warmth of her body pressed against his back. He released the pistol's safety mechanism.

Frosty air bombarded him, and his bare feet sank into snow. Thank heavens it'd been so cold that he and Beth had put on clothes before falling asleep in front of the fire. They'd saved precious time.

Impossible to see more than a few feet ahead, but there was no sign of anyone and no car in sight. Had he imagined the noise? Could it have been an animal rather than a human? Slowly, he advanced to the side of the cabin, Beth at his back with her shotgun at the ready.

An explosion of shattered glass broke the night's eerie silence. Sammy ran toward the back of the cabin, gun raised. The shadows shifted, and he made out a large figure running toward the tree line that bordered the county road. The bedroom window was broken.

"Halt!" he shouted. The figure kept running. No way he could see well enough to land a shot, but Sammy fired his pistol in the air, hoping it would scare the man into surrender.

It did not.

Sammy gave chase, his mind racing as fast as his feet running in the freezing snow. Had the attacker heard them approach? Why hadn't he entered the cabin through the broken window. Unless…

He reached out an arm for Beth, relieved when he made contact with the solid strength of her body. "Get down!"

An explosion shook the ground at his feet as he dropped to his knees and then laid his body above Beth's. His ears rang with the sound of an incendiary pipe bomb exploding. Fire billowed from the cabin, illuminating the sky like lightning. Debris flew through the wind— wood, glass and ash. The snow reflected the giant leaping flames, giving the impression of molten lava spilling on the ground.

Sammy tore his eyes from the horrific damage and scanned the area, eyes peeled for any sight of the attacker returning or any accomplices lurking nearby.

From up the road, the beam of car headlights cut through the darkness.

"They're getting away!" Beth said, pushing him off and scrambling to her feet. "We've got to stop them."

She ran toward the cabin, and he caught up to her, tugging at her arm. "Hurry," she urged. "Get the car keys. We can't let them escape."

"I'll get them. You wait here."

"I can help you search."

"Too dangerous."

Without waiting for an argument, he ran past her. Sammy pulled off his T-shirt and covered his mouth and nose. At the gaping door, precariously tilted to the right, he blinked against the plumes of ash and smoke. His keys, cell phone and two-way radio were located on the far left end of the den on the coffee table they'd pushed against the wall last night so they could sleep in front of the fire. Among other things they'd done there. If they hadn't made love and slept together, if Beth had slept in the bedroom as she had the previous night, she'd be dead.

A chill racked his body—one that had nothing to do with winter. His professional training kicked in. *Deal with that later; there's work to be done.* He sucked in a chest full of air and entered the smoky cabin. Acrid fumes assaulted his nose and eyes. Blinking wildly, he put one hand along the wall to move forward without becoming disoriented by the thick curtain of smoke. Sammy crouched low and tried to ignore the heat emanating from the blistered wood that burned his hand and feet.

Even though he tried not to take deep breaths, smoke filled his lungs and he coughed, struggling for oxygen. The hair on his arms bristled painfully from the heat. Fire roared and crackled and pieces of wood haphazardly fell from the ceiling.

Just a few more steps.

Pain shot through the arch of his right foot as a large glass shard cut through flesh. Sammy kept going. He had no choice; they had to pursue whoever had tried to kill them. This might be their only chance to capture the bastard.

He felt the edge of the coffee table before he saw it. Would the radio and phones already be destroyed by heat and smoke? They were fiery in his palms, but he pocketed the items. Where were those damn keys? He brushed the surface of the table, scorching the bare skin of his right forearm. Nothing. They must have fallen on the floor. Still keeping one hand in contact with the wall, he got on all fours and swept his free hand along the floor until they brushed against jagged metal.

Feeling victorious, he stuffed them in his pocket and started to rise back up on his feet. His head bumped against something solid. The easel clattered to the ground.

Beth's paintings! Her stunning, elegant snowscapes.

Violent coughing seized his lungs. *Get out*, brain and body urged. But he couldn't let Beth's art burn to smithereens. All that work, all that beauty. He slid his left foot over until it thumped against the wall, his anchor in the sea of flames and smoke, and then he gathered the canvases that had fallen to the ground, praying that the thick cloth she'd thrown over the paintings had kept her work from being destroyed.

A large beam fell from the ceiling, landing only a foot from where he stood. It was past time to get the hell out of the cabin. Sammy sprinted toward the door, enduring the gauntlet of the hot floor littered with broken glass. At last he hobbled outside and gulped crisp mountain air down his parched lungs. Snow numbed the bottoms of his burning feet that were laced with gashes.

He thrust the paintings into Beth's arms and turned back to make a mad dash for their jackets and shoes, but the singed door frame buckled, and the overhead wooden strip of the frame dangled precariously in the opening.

Barefoot it was.

And there was no time to waste if they wanted to catch a killer.

Chapter Ten

Beth gaped as Sammy shoved her oil paintings into her arms. She hadn't given them a moment's thought. After all, how many had she painted over the years? Dozens and dozens. And although painting was her profession— one of the ways she made a living, along with teaching art—no one would ever believe her work so valuable that they would risk death by fire to save them.

Not her father, who, though proud, had viewed her "hobby" with an indulgence she'd found more condescending than appreciative,

Not Cynthia, who filtered everything and everybody through the lens of their monetary value.

Not Aiden, who mostly regarded the world from the same perspective as his mother, mixed with an intellectual vigor that her father had favored and encouraged.

If Mom had lived, Beth felt certain she would

have understood and appreciated her daughter's artistic success, modest though it was. Mom had always insisted on Beth receiving art lessons and had proudly displayed her childhood drawings. But Mom had died a long, long time ago and Beth still missed her love and encouragement. Since a young teen, she'd felt like a misunderstood, undervalued changeling in the Wynngate family.

And then there was Sammy. The man who had arrested her as a teenager. The man she'd blamed for over a decade for exiling her from her family. She'd misjudged him as uncaring, arrogant.

Beth forgot the horrific explosion, the burning cabin her father had loved, the chill seeping in her bones and bare feet, and the knowledge that someone was trying to kill her. There was only Sammy, covered with ash and grime, rescuing her canvases as though Dad's cabin was a museum on fire and her work was Van Gogh's.

She couldn't move. Couldn't speak past the pinch in her heart.

"Let's go!" Sammy ran past her, limping and still coughing violently.

Beth blinked away the hot tears that had unexpectedly arisen. "You're hurt. I'll drive."

Without argument, Sammy dug in his jeans pocket and tossed her the keys. Beth tossed her paintings in the back seat, got in and started the motor. It took a couple of seconds to find the light switch on the dashboard panel and get her bearings with a strange vehicle, then the Jeep lurched forward as she hit the accelerator. She bounced in her seat as they crossed over the uneven land of the small clearing and then onto a dirt road. Only one way out of here and then onto the main road.

She had to catch up to the bomber. If they didn't, she could never feel safe again. Each attack grew more aggressive. Next time, she might not escape with her life. How the hell had he found them out here? Was it Dorsey? Sammy had been right. Rayna had no influence on her son—either that, or she hadn't even tried to get through to him.

"Maybe I should have wired that fifty thousand dollars," she said, finding and switching to bright lights. "Or tried to promise them I would get them the money somehow. If I had, they might not have come after me tonight."

"Hell, no! You can't deal with criminals that way." Sammy fiddled with a dial and a blast of welcome heat fanned her chilled body. "It's a game you'd never win."

Snow silently whirled through the wind. Pine trees crowded the road alongside of the Jeep. They made it to the paved county road. In the distance, she caught the elliptical beam of headlights rounding a curve. The attacker was heading north.

Beth stayed focused on the twin rays of headlights ahead, steadily gaining on the bomber. Did he know they were in pursuit? She barely registered Sammy's ongoing radio conversation as he called in their location and requested backup. The static stop-and-go talking provided a comforting backdrop of noise as she sped down the lonely stretch of pavement in the moonlight.

Miles flew past, and although she seemed to be gaining on the vehicle ahead, it stayed frustratingly out of eyesight. She wanted that tag number. She wanted an arrest. She wanted this ordeal to be over. Tonight. Not only for herself, but for her family and for Sammy. No one in her circle was safe.

The county road began to twist as they headed back up the mountain and the elevation rose. With every turn and climb, the wind howled stronger. The snow seemed to swirl faster, and the trees flashed by at an alarming rate. But Beth drove on, jaw clenched with determination even as her fingers painfully clenched the steering wheel. Her bare feet vibrated with the rumble of the Jeep's engine as it strained under the demanding conditions.

Ahead, she caught a glimpse of a yellow Dodge truck. A little closer and they'd have the tag number. But her jubilation was short-lived as the truck turned sharply onto GA 180—Georgia's own deadly version of the Tail of the Dragon roadway. Bad enough during the day when motorcyclists and other thrill seekers often raced down it. But on a snowy winter night? Despite the continued blast of the heater, her whole body began to tremble.

"We don't have to chase him down the mountain," Sammy said. "If we're lucky, one of our cops might get here in time to put up a roadblock."

If they were lucky. Right now, she didn't feel like Lady Luck was on her side. "I'm not quitting," she told Sammy.

"Want me to drive?"

"There's no time to switch places. We could lose him." Before she could change her mind, Beth turned the Jeep onto GA 180. At least she knew what to expect—a road as narrow as the width of a driveway with miles of blind turns and steep elevation changes. As a teenager, she'd driven down it a time or two, only to prove to Aiden that she wasn't a chicken. Whoever they were pursuing must also be a local to even attempt the ride.

She began the descent down the Tail of the

Dragon. At the first blind turn, the Jeep's tires skidded on a sudden icy patch and the vehicle slid several feet to the very edge of the bank. Beth's heart beat painfully against her ribs, even after she righted course and prepared for the next turn.

"Careful there," Sammy said tightly. "Didn't know your real name was Mrs. Mario Andretti."

"Who?"

"Andretti. A legendary race car driver."

Beth slowed a fraction. The only worse outcome than the bomber escaping them would be if she crashed the Jeep. Multiple wooden cross memorials alongside the road were a silent testament to the danger.

The yellow truck ahead didn't slow. Seemed the bomber was more desperate to escape them than they were to capture him and demand answers. At the next sharp curve, the truck veered so close to the edge of the cliff that it clipped the guardrail. The sound of tire squeals and grinding metal screamed through the snowy gales.

Down, down she drove, frustrated at the growing distance between the Jeep and the truck but too cautious to try and gain on it again.

"You're doing a great job," Sammy said

softly. "We're over the halfway point down now. It's almost over."

"It won't be over until we get—"

Another squeal of tires filled the air—long and shrill. The truck's driver must have lost control of his vehicle. Beth tapped on the brakes, not knowing what to expect when she emerged from the blind curve. If the driver had crashed into the mountain wall on the right, his truck might be flung back onto the middle of the road, a deadly obstruction for their on-coming Jeep.

She rounded the bend—to see her worst fear come true. The truck slammed into the mountain with a deafening crash. Sparks mingled with snow and metal debris flew through the air like firecracker missiles.

"Look out!" Sammy shouted.

This was no time for mere brake-tapping. "Hold tight," she warned, slamming her foot on the brake, arms clenched to the steering wheel in a death grip as she braced for possible impact.

The truck spun out of control and back toward the guardrail. More grinding of metal on metal ensued and an unmistakable human wail of terror rent the air.

The Jeep grounded to a sudden halt, in time for front-row viewing to a nightmare. The truck toppled over the rail, flipping once before disappearing into darkness. But she heard the crash from the bottom of the mountain as it landed once, then twice, and finally a third time. With each thunderous clap of the tumbling truck, Beth winced. Sammy was back on the two-way radio, barking out their location and requesting an ambulance. Again her body shook so hard that her teeth began to chatter. Sammy flung an arm over her shoulders and squeezed her tight. The solid strength of his arms comforted her and warmed the chilly despair that had momentarily overtaken her body.

"You did great, Beth. I couldn't have asked for a better partner tonight. Help's on the way."

Before she could do more than nod in reply, an explosion blasted from below. Tall flames burst high in a column of orange flares. Sirens wailed in the distance. Sammy flung open the passenger door.

"What are you doing?" she cried in surprise. "You can't go out there. You're not even wearing shoes!"

Sammy's gaze flicked to the back seat and he leaned over, plucking a towel and a jacket from a gym bag. He hastily pulled out the larger shards in his feet, then wrapped each item on a foot for makeshift shoes. "Keep the headlights pointed straight ahead," he instructed. "They know we're here by mile marker eight. I'm just going to stand by the edge of the road and take a quick look."

The door shut behind him and she watched as he picked his way through the haphazardly strewn metal wreckage. A compulsion to see the burning truck overcame her common sense. She opened the Jeep door and Sammy spun around.

"Don't come out here. There's glass everywhere."

"I want to see."

He shook his head and then crossed over to her. "Okay. Just for a minute," he said, putting an arm under her thighs and then lifting her out of the vehicle. She leaned into his solid warmth as the mountain wind whipped around them. He only took a few steps before stopping, mere inches from the smashed-in guardrail.

The twisted metal hull of the truck was engulfed by flames. Black plumes of smoke spiraled among the fire. For the second time tonight, the smell of gasoline permeated the air. But now the acrid scent of scorched rubber mixed with the fuel. The Tail of the Dragon was breathing fire tonight as it claimed yet another victim.

"He couldn't have survived," she whispered.

"No," he grimly agreed. "So much for that lead."

His harsh words weighed on her. "But won't you be able to discover who that man was? Or at least who owned the truck?"

"We will."

"Then we'll be closer to an answer."

Blue lights and sirens snaked up the mountain. Sammy carried her back to the Jeep, and she waited inside as he met with law enforcement officers. EMTs scrambled from an ambulance with stretchers and headed down the mountain. Firefighters joined them and somehow the dark corner of the mountain was flooded with light in all directions as emergency responders set to work. Sammy emerged from the crowd of people and returned to the Jeep, an EMT by his side.

"You need to go with Adam," Sammy told her gently. "He'll take you to the Elmore Community Hospital. You need to be checked for shock and to make sure you don't have any serious wounds."

"Wounds?" she asked blankly.

"You're covered with cuts," he explained.

She glanced down, surprised at the number of bloody scratches crisscrossing her arms and legs. "How…"

"When the bomb went off, debris flew everywhere. You've been too pumped with adrenaline to notice."

"What about you? You've been limping. Did you burn your feet in the fire?"

"I'll be fine—"

"What's this?" A deep voice interrupted. "Are you injured, Sammy?" Sheriff Harlan Sampson suddenly stood beside them, frowning and surveying them with his hands on his hips.

"It's not bad, mostly a gash on one foot," Sammy said, obviously trying to minimize the injury.

Harlan cocked his head toward the ambulance. "Go get it looked at."

"But you need my report and—"

"That can wait. We have enough information for tonight. We'll get your car down the mountain for you." Harlan glanced at her thoughtfully. "Besides, someone needs to watch out for Ms. Wynngate at the hospital. My wife would never forgive me if something happened to her friend."

His manner was not unkind, but Beth suddenly felt a crushing weight on her chest. She'd placed his officer in danger. Harlan most likely would love to see her hightail it back to Boston, far away from his department's responsibility. Far away from Lilah. Not that she couldn't understand his feelings. Danger followed wherever she roamed, no matter how far or remote the location.

She followed Sammy into the back of another officer's cruiser, which rushed them to the hospital. Sammy's foot required stitches and by the time they were fully examined and cleaned up, dawn streaked the sky. Even though the adrenaline had left her body, she felt oddly restless and not in the least tired.

Lilah burst through the examination room, carrying several large plastic bags. She dropped them to the floor and enveloped Beth in a bear hug. "Are you okay? Harlan told me what happened." Lilah stepped back and appraised her. "You look horrible."

"Why, thank you," Beth said, attempting a smile.

"You know what I mean." Lilah retrieved one of the fallen bags and handed it to her. "I brought clean clothes for you." She shoved the other bag at Sammy. "And for you. I believe you and Harlan are about the same size, so these should fit."

"I can't wait to change out of these stinky clothes," Beth said, wondering if the stench of smoke would ever leave her nostrils.

"Ditto," Sammy echoed, hobbling over to the men's room to change.

Lilah followed her into the ladies' bathroom. "So what's the game plan now? You and Sammy should come stay with us until all this mess blows over."

Beth's gaze involuntarily slid to Lilah's pregnant belly. Much as she would enjoy staying at Lilah's, she couldn't put her friend in danger. "I've worked it out already. Aiden returned early from his trip and insisted I come stay with him a few days until Lambert's locked up."

After the abysmal failure of the remote cabin to keep her safe, the busy high-rise condo bustling with people felt infinitely more secure. At least someone would hear her scream if Lambert attacked.

Lilah stuffed the smoke-ruined clothes in an empty plastic bag as Beth changed into jeans and a sweater. "I'll wash these for you," Lilah offered.

"Those old things? Don't bother. Just dump them in the trash can."

Lilah pulled a pair of sneakers and slippers from the bag. "My shoes might be a size too small for you, if I remember right. If nothing else, you can wear these bedroom slippers and stop somewhere on the way to buy a new pair of shoes."

Beth didn't even try the sneakers, opting for

the warm, furry slippers. "Thanks, Lilah. I'll return everything to you later."

Lilah waved a dismissive hand. "Is Sammy driving you to Aiden's place?"

"Your husband made sure his car was brought to the hospital. And Sammy insisted on taking me."

"Might be a good idea." Lilah shook her head and held open the bathroom door. "Still can't get over that they tried to kill you."

"They?" Beth's brow furrowed. Lilah must be speaking of the Lambert family in general.

"Yeah. Those two whose bodies the cops found last night. They'd been flung a good distance from the truck."

It hadn't even occurred to her there would be more than the lone driver behind the attack. "So one of them threw the pipe bomb while another waited in a getaway truck?"

"That's what Harlan speculates."

It felt as though a cold ice cube suddenly slivered down her spine. The whole thing had been so…premeditated. "Wonder if one of the men was the same guy who threatened me in town yesterday."

"Maybe. I wouldn't put anything past Marty Upshaw."

Beth stepped into the brightly lit hospital hallway. Now that she'd donned fresh clothes, the scent of smoke was replaced by an antiseptic zing in the air. "And who did the other body belong to?"

Lilah's brows rose. "You haven't heard yet?"

A knot of dread formed in her stomach. Judging by Lilah's reaction, this person might have been someone she'd known. "Who?" she whispered.

"Abbie Fenton."

Chapter Eleven

Sammy stepped off the elevator, Beth's suitcases in each of his hands. It had been quick work gathering her clothes and toiletries from the Wynngate house before the short drive to Atlanta. He followed her down a long hallway in Aiden's condo building, impressed that even this utilitarian part of the building had a luxurious feel, with chandeliers, plush carpeting and a view of downtown from floor-to-ceiling windows that banked both ends of the hall. Beth, of course, paid it no mind as she strode to Aiden's door and rang the bell.

Unease niggled the back of his mind. With all the danger and forced intimacy between them, he'd pushed away the realization of how different their social statuses were. A blue-collar man like himself would be a real step down in the world inhabited by the Wynngates and others with their wealth.

Steps sounded from the opposite side of the

door and he wondered how his old friend would greet him. It'd been at least four or five years since they'd last met. The encounter had felt awkward for Sammy and he suspected it had for Aiden, as well. After only a minute of reminiscing on old times, he'd found himself floundering in the conversation. There was no longer a common ground between them.

The door flung open, and Aiden filled the doorway with his tall, charismatic presence, throwing Sammy a grin as he hugged Beth in welcome. "You always bring the excitement when you visit us," he teased.

"Sure you don't mind me crashing a few days?"

"Don't be silly. 'Course not." Aiden thrust out his hand to Sammy. "How you doing, buddy?"

"Fine," he answered, as though he and Beth hadn't been through hell all last night.

Aiden opened the door all the way and gestured them inside. The industrial, minimalistic feel of the place struck Sammy as coldly formal. Everything was gray or dull white. The room would be much improved if Beth's colorful paintings graced the stark walls. Odd that her brother didn't display any of them, but he supposed everyone should be allowed to live with their own tastes in their own home. Beth stood beside him and leaned into him, resting her head against his chest. He slung an arm over her shoulder and gave her a reassuring squeeze. The worst was over. Now they needed to rest and recoup.

If Aiden wondered about the connection between his sister and old friend, he didn't remark on it. "You both must be dead on your feet," he said. "Come on in and sit down."

"That's okay. I should be going—"

"Nonsense."

Beth pleaded with her eyes. "You should rest before driving back to Lavender Mountain. Maybe even take a nap?"

"Good idea," Aiden said approvingly. "I have a couple of empty guest rooms. Stay as long as you want."

"No, I really need to get some paperwork done today," he argued. Not to mention there were so many angles he wanted to follow up on. With any luck, Charlotte might have unearthed something useful in the investigation. He could use a bit of good news right about now.

"At least sit down and drink some coffee," Beth urged.

Aiden clapped his hands together. "Excellent idea. I have an espresso machine that makes a mean cup of joe."

Of course he did. Sammy would have preferred a soda, but he gave Aiden a nod. "Sounds good."

Beth lifted the two suitcases sitting by the doorway. "If you don't mind, I'm going to take a quick shower."

He needed one, as well, but he'd wait until he got home. Sammy followed Aiden into the kitchen with its broad expanse of marble countertops and stainless steel appliances. "Nice place," he commented.

"Isn't it?" Aiden agreed with an appreciative smile. "And you should see the gym and pool downstairs. We even have an indoor racquetball court." He beamed with pride as he ground fresh coffee beans and then emptied them into a complicated-looking machine. "There's even a five-star restaurant on the lobby level that delivers room service on nights I'm too beat to cook or go out. Best of all, my office is less than a quarter mile away. So convenient."

"Must be nice," he offered, watching as Aiden fussed with the espresso maker and retrieved glass cups from a cabinet. From the bank of windows over the sink, he could see a line of cars inching forward on the bypass. Good thing Aiden lived so close to his law firm. Otherwise, the commute would be a bitch.

No thanks. He'd take the slow pace of Lavender Mountain any day. Frowning, Sammy eyed the button-down shirt and tailored gray pants Aiden wore. "Are you going back to work today? I thought you were still on vacation."

"Vacation?" He barked out a laugh. "Is that what Beth told you? I've been on a business trip. No rest when you're the boss. But don't worry, I can work here at home the next few days while y'all get this situation sorted. Any idea when they might arrest Lambert?"

Aiden filled both their cups and pointed at the cream and sugar by the machine.

"Atlanta PD has an APB out on him. Could be any minute now."

Aiden shook his head. "Can't imagine why anyone would want to hurt my sister. Are the Lamberts trying to kidnap Beth and hold her for ransom? Is that the theory?"

"Maybe." If Beth hadn't volunteered more information, he certainly wouldn't. Sammy sipped the coffee. For all the elegant preparation and presentation, it tasted like any old cup of black coffee. Maybe his taste buds, like his life in general, lacked sophistication.

"She'll be safe with me, although we might drive each other up the wall if we're home alone together all day every day." Aiden chuckled. "Between us, Beth can be pretty flaky. If you know what I mean."

He frowned. "No, I don't know what you

mean. She seems extremely levelheaded to me. Brave, too."

"Oh, sure, sure," Aiden said placatingly. "But you don't know her as well as I do. She's a typical artist. Kind of moody and always has her head in the clouds. It's cute at first, but it wears thin after a while."

"In what way?" Sammy asked, unable to keep the sharp edge out of his voice.

"Don't get me wrong, she's my sister and I love her of course, but she can be overly dramatic. Not to mention a bit spoiled, too. The judge sent her to the finest schools and left her a substantial inheritance. And what does she have to show for it? A job teaching art to middle schoolers." He gave a smug snicker.

"There's nothing wrong with the teaching profession. And Beth happens to be a highly talented painter."

Aiden sipped his coffee and then set it down. "She's a dilettante. By now, she should be seeing someone in our crowd or going to graduate school and learning a real profession."

Anger burned his cheeks and the nape of his neck. Could Aiden have been more obvious in his disapproval of his and Beth's attraction? With one broad stroke, he'd managed to insult Beth as a flighty no-talent hack and himself as a poor, unacceptable match for a member of the Wynngate family.

"Maybe what Beth wants isn't the same as what you believe she needs," Sammy said, striving to keep his anger in check. "And give her a little credit. Beth is a smart, talented and capable woman who makes her own decisions."

Aiden frowned. "You misunderstand what I'm saying. I'm only—"

A sharp voice sounded from behind. "Your message was unmistakable." Beth glared at her brother, pushing back a lock of wet hair from her face. "Nice to know your real opinion of me—an overly dramatic, spoiled dilettante."

"You're twisting my words," he protested. "And how long have you been eavesdropping?

"I'm repeating exactly what you said. And I couldn't help but overhear as I walked over."

"C'mon, Beth, I'm sorry. Don't be so sensitive. I didn't mean anything by it."

A bitter laugh escaped her mouth. "Of course you meant something by it. And you insulted Sammy, too. Apologize to him."

Although gratified at Beth's quick defense, Sammy didn't want to cause trouble between her and her brother. "It's okay," he said quickly.

Aiden's face flushed crimson and he didn't spare Sammy a glance. "You're making a big deal out of nothing," he insisted.

"You implied he was unsuitable. Not good enough for a Wynngate."

"I didn't say that." Again Aiden refused to look him in the eye.

"Bad enough you put me down, but I'm not going to stand by and let you do the same with my friends. At least Sammy hasn't come to me with his hands out, asking to borrow money."

"I asked if you wanted to invest in my new law firm. Not to borrow." Aiden carefully set his coffee cup on the counter. "There's a big difference. It's not like you don't have the money."

Sammy started to ease out of the kitchen. This was family business and he didn't belong.

"And I gladly lent you thousands of dollars," Beth said, her voice calmer now. "This isn't about the money. It's about respect."

Aiden held up his hands, palms out. "You're right. I don't want to argue. Sammy, don't leave. Seems I owe you an apology. No offense, okay?"

"Sure," Sammy said, not believing for a second that Aiden was sincere, but to ease Beth's feelings. She'd been through enough the last few days without him contributing to this sibling conflict. So what if Aiden looked down his patrician nose at him? He really didn't give a damn. Their friendship had been over for years.

"See? Sammy's fine. And I promise, you'll get your money back within the year. With interest."

Sammy cleared his throat. "Guess I'll be heading down the road. Thanks for letting Beth stay with you a few days, Aiden."

"My pleasure—"

"I'm not staying." Beth strode out of the kitchen and headed for the door.

Aiden trailed after her. "But—I thought you needed a safe place to stay."

Sammy sighed. He couldn't blame Beth for not wanting to hide out here. But where could she go now that was safe? She'd already refused to stay with him, and her stepmother obviously didn't want Beth at her place or Beth would have gone there.

Beth snatched her bags from one of the bedrooms and reemerged with her face still set in stony resolve, Aiden at her heels and trying to convince her not to leave. Sammy held the door open and Beth faced her brother one last time. "We'll talk later. I'm too upset right now. Bye, Aiden."

Sammy gave a quick nod to the chagrined Aiden and they silently proceeded to the elevator. Once the doors closed behind them, Beth gave him a rueful smile. "Sorry you had to see that. It was ugly, wasn't it?"

"A little. Can't say I blame you for walking out, but now we have to figure out our next move. Have you changed your mind about staying with me in Lavender Mountain? I can provide 24/7 police protection."

"No. I won't put you in that kind of danger. Plus, there's too many eyes in that town. Word would get around where I'm staying."

"Let me decide about the risk. My main concern is your protection. I don't want anything to happen to you."

Chapter Twelve

Sammy's worry about her safety thawed the chill in her heart left from Aiden's harsh words. But then, how much was merely professional concern on his part? Couldn't look good on a deputy sheriff's record to have someone hurt while under his protection. Beth shook off the depressing thought, her usual optimism starting to surface. A good breakfast and a few hours' sleep in her favorite hotel was in order.

"This is it," she announced. "Pull up to the lobby entrance and let's spring for valet service."

"Fancy," Sammy commented as he whipped the Jeep to the door.

The downtown W Hotel gleamed like a skyscraper diamond in the morning sunshine— all glass and chrome, a tall beacon promising warmth and comfort. It was her favorite place to stay in the city. On annual home visits, she often opted to stay at the W in a private suite instead of with family. That way she, Cynthia and Aiden didn't get into each other's hair too much.

With quick and courteous efficiency, they were ushered into the studio suite she preferred. The corner room featured floor-to-ceiling windows that offered stunning views of Atlanta. The energy of the city was also captured in the vibrant turquoise-and-magenta color scheme that clicked with her artist's eye.

"This is amazing," Sammy said, surveying the room. The dazed, appreciative expression on his face spoke volumes. Luxury suites probably weren't much on his radar, living as he did on a deputy sheriff's salary. She hoped she hadn't made him uncomfortable. Perhaps this wasn't the best choice after Aiden's so-recent snobby remarks. Although she'd inherited a substantial amount of money from her parents, she wasn't one to flaunt her wealth. But after everything they'd been through last night, she wanted to treat them both to the very best.

Beth flopped onto the king-size bed and sought to put him at ease. "I hope you love it here as much as I do. It's 'old-fashioned Southern hospitality meets modern chic meets artistic flair.'"

"I suppose this room will be okay," he remarked dryly. "Although I could do without the hot-pink blanket and pillows."

"Think of it as a rich shade of magenta, not pink."

"Tell it to my hormones. My testosterone level dropped the moment I saw it."

Beth laughed and sprang to her feet. "Let's order room service for breakfast and then catch a nap."

"I really should head back to the station. Harlan will be expecting a report by the end of the day."

"Harlan would expect you to rest and then do whatever you have to do. Besides, you can order a laptop brought here from the hotel's business center and email a report. No need to drive all the way back to Lavender Mountain."

"They would do that?" he asked in surprise.

"Of course. Welcome to the twenty-first century."

"The technology isn't what surprised me. I'm talking about the service. You don't get that at the local motel chains I use."

She searched his face for a hint of rancor but, to her relief, found none. Treating Sammy to the very best was going to be fun. In short order, they were seated at the window table and dining on a brunch of shrimp and grits, fried green tomatoes and bacon biscuits. The coziness felt extra intimate as they watched office workers and shoppers crowding the streets below under a light dusting of snow.

Once their hunger was sated, a different physical appetite was aroused. His eyes blazed across the table at her as he slowly set his fork down. Wordlessly, Sammy took her hand and led her to bed. That large luscious bed with its soft mattress—a stark contrast to the hard floor of the cabin where they'd made love last night. Not that she was complaining. She'd always treasure the memory of discovering the feel of his strong, sleek body and the taste of his mouth as the fireplace crackled in the background.

Beth never imagined it possible but making love to Sammy the second time around was even more exciting than the first. He kissed and touched her in just the right places, already an expert on her sensual desires. Need welled in her, frantic and desperate until at last he entered her. She met each thrust with wild abandon. Pleasure at last ripped through her and she held on to him as the tremors subsided. Only then did he allow his own orgasm and she marveled at what a skillful and tender lover Sammy was.

The long, sleepless hours finally caught up to her. Beth closed her eyes and snuggled into Sammy's warm arms, drifting into welcome slumber.

A cell phone rang, jarring her out of sleep. The illusion of safety and isolation from the rest of the world lifted in an instant. Sammy rolled away from her and picked the phone up off the nightstand.

"Armstrong, here." A pause and then he sat up, all business. "You've got him? I'll be right down."

"What is it?" she asked breathlessly. "Has Lambert been found?"

"Found and arrested. Atlanta PD are holding him at their midtown station." Sammy slid out of bed and picked up his clothes lying on the floor. "Can't wait to interrogate the little bastard."

Beth got out of bed and snatched up her clothes, as well. "I'll go with you."

"No need. Go back to sleep. I could be gone for hours." He quickly began dressing.

She paused, about to pull her T-shirt over her head. "Are you sure?"

"Positive." He grinned and drew her in for a brief, fierce kiss. "You're safe now," he proclaimed. "We're shutting Lambert and the rest of his family down. It's finally over, Beth."

Just that quickly. It was almost hard to take in. "Safe," she echoed. "I like the sound of that."

Sammy grabbed his jacket. "Let's celebrate when I get back. Anywhere you want to go." He gestured at the windows. Already, lights twinkled in the gathering dusk. "The city's finest dining and entertainment. You decide."

"Perfect."

With a quick wave, he left, and the door shut behind him, only to open a second later. "Dead bolt the lock behind me."

"Thought I was safe," she said with a laugh.

"Can't be too careful."

Once a cop, always a cop. Although Beth couldn't say she minded his attention and concern. She'd lived alone too long not to appreciate the caring behind the admonitions. Dutifully, she crossed to the door and secured the lock. Turning around, she faced the rumpled bed where they'd just made love. Should she crawl back in and catch more sleep?

The idea had no appeal. She was too excited to go back to sleep. At the windows, she glimpsed the valet bringing around the Jeep and the slight limp in Sammy's step where he'd had stitches. He drove off and she sighed, wishing she'd insisted on going with him. Although, what good would that do? She wasn't a cop and they wouldn't let her listen in on the interrogation. She'd be stuck sitting in the dismal precinct atmosphere for at least a couple of hours sipping bad coffee and munching vending machine potato chips.

Beth sat in a turquoise-and-pink chair by the window and gazed at the view. The blue-top dome of the Polaris lounge caught her eye. Instantly, her mouth watered with the remembered taste of the peach frozen daiquiri they were famous for making. The place had its own bee garden to harvest honey for their handcrafted libations. Plus, the domed restaurant atop the Hyatt Regency rotated, offering spectacular views of Atlanta at night. Sammy might get a kick out of the fresh vegetables grown on their rooftop garden.

Decision made, Beth called and made a reservation. If Sammy had time tomorrow, they could extend their celebration and spend the day at the Georgia Aquarium. She glanced at the time on her cell phone, noting that only twenty minutes had passed since Sammy left. She paced the room, wondering what Dorsey Lambert was telling the police. Would he rat out members of his family he'd recruited to help him? She thought of Abbie. So young to have died. The violence of the truck crash played out in her mind—the sound of it as it flipped and rolled down rocky mountain terrain and then burst into flames. In a way, the sights and sounds of the crash made her cringe as much as the exploding pipe bomb in the cabin. At least that disaster had been unexpected. They'd never seen it coming. But that icy race down the Tail of the Dragon had seemed to go on for hours and hours.

At last she managed to rest for a while in the comfortable chair, even dozing a little as she waited for Sammy's return. She didn't know how long she conked out but eventually she roused, blinking her eyes fast to reorient herself.

From the hallway, an elevator door pinged open and shut. It was a busy time of day for guests to head out for cocktails and dinner. More footsteps shuffled outside and then came to an abrupt halt by her room. Beneath the door slat, a pair of dark men's shoes blocked the hall light. The lock jiggled. Her heart hammered, and her throat went dry.

A drunken businessman mistaking her room for his?

A sharp rap hammered the door. Beth didn't move. Didn't speak. Maybe whoever was out there would realize his mistake and just go away.

Another loud knock. *You're safe now*, Sammy had said. She'd known it was too good to be true.

Beth grabbed her cell phone and punched in 9-1-1 with trembling fingers. If whoever was

out there tried to break down the door, she'd
hit the call button.

"Beth?" a deep voice called out. "Beth, are
you in there?"

"Wh-who is it?" she asked, a hand at her throat.

"It's me, Aiden. Come to apologize. Let me in."

Aiden. A tsunami of relief swooshed through
her body and her knees threatened to buckle.
She grabbed onto a chair to keep from falling
to the floor. Drawing a deep breath, she hurried
to the door and flung it open. Aiden grinned
down, holding up a bottle of merlot. "I knew
you'd be at this place. Figured I'd bribe you to
let me in with your favorite wine."

She gave a weak laugh. "You scared the hell
out of me. Come on in."

Aiden sauntered inside and surveyed the
room. "Nice digs. You always liked this place.
Where's Sammy?"

"At the police station." She shut the door and
reset the dead bolt. "They called not thirty minutes ago saying they had Dorsey Lambert in
custody. Sammy will be back before too long."

"They've got Lambert? That's fantastic
news! Let's have a drink and toast an excellent bit of police work."

"You didn't have to come bearing gifts," she admonished, though secretly glad for the company.

Aiden set to work, gathering two crystal

glasses from the kitchenette and setting them on the table. He popped the cork and began to pour.

"I'll join you in a second," she said.

Beth scurried into the bathroom and winced at her reflection. As she suspected, the mussed hair and streaked mascara made it appear as though she'd just rolled out of bed—after being thoroughly pleasured by a lover. Which she was. But she didn't need to parade that fact in front of her brother, because…just *eww*, he was her brother. Hastily, she brushed her hair and swiped at the makeup under her eyes. Much better.

When she returned to the table, Aiden was already seated, drinking wine. He gestured to the other poured glass and she gratefully sipped. The merlot was smooth and flavorful but a bit on the dry side, with the faintest afternote of bitter. Still, it was delicious and just what she needed after the last few harrowing days. If only Sammy was here to join them, the evening would be perfect.

"You've been through a hell of an ordeal, haven't you?" Aiden's dark brown eyes were warm with concern. "And then I heaped more trouble on you when you came to me for help. I was way out of line. I'm really sorry. Forgive me?"

"Of course." And she meant it. The Aiden

seated across from her was her brother of old, his refreshing tenderness a quality that always helped brush over Cynthia's sometimes cutting indifference.

Aiden glanced at his expensive watch. "How long before Sammy returns? An hour? Two hours?"

"Two at the most. I'm hoping he'll be back within the hour."

"Heading home when he returns?"

"Nope. Going out to celebrate. Come with us for cocktails and dinner at the Polaris."

"Maybe."

"Anything wrong?" she asked. "You seem on edge this evening."

"No, no. Everything's fine. Matter of fact, I've got some good news, too."

More good news. Tonight was certainly her lucky night. Everything was nicely turning around. "Tell me."

Aiden raised his glass. "Drink up first."

Beth took another long sip. "Now what's up?"

"My firm's finally in the black. We got a large civil suit settlement and several more excellent prospects lined up. Wynngate LLC is starting to attract prominent customers."

Beth flushed with pride that her family's name was being honored by her stepbrother's firm. Dad had adopted Aiden when he married Cynthia and Aiden had always aspired to follow in his footsteps. "That's great. I'm so proud of you, Aiden. I knew you'd make a success of it."

When he'd first approached her six months ago to invest in his new criminal defense law firm, she'd had a few misgivings. Particularly when she heard the office would be in a new, swanky building situated in the trendy Buckhead area of the city. "Takes money to make money," Aiden had assured her. And spent money he had. Her brother was always wining and dining potential clients, but it looked as though the hard work was finally paying off.

Aiden raised his glass and pointedly looked at hers. Beth obligingly took another swallow.

"Best of all," he continued, "I should be able to repay you—with interest—by the first of the year."

Beth tried not to show her relief, afraid Aiden would take it as a lack of faith in his abilities. But more than the money, she wanted their sibling relationship unencumbered by awkwardness over the loan.

He clinked his glass with hers and they toasted his good fortune. Aiden picked up the merlot bottle and refilled her glass.

"I'm not sure I should have another," she

protested. "My heart's set on a peach daiquiri later."

"Lighten up," he said with a laugh. "You deserve this. And I certainly don't want to drink alone."

A second glass of wine never hurt anybody. Beth shrugged and took another sip from the full glass. Already, her body seemed to be floating and her head swam. With shaking hands, she carefully set the goblet on the table, oddly mesmerized by the shimmer of the crimson liquid under the lamp.

"No more for me," she stated with an uneasy laugh.

"Well, you're no fun. I bought this merlot just for you."

"Doesn't mean I can drink it all in one sitting."

"That's my Beth. Always were a bit of a spoilsport. Never one to party hard like me and my friends."

And yet, she was the one who had paid the price years ago when his friends had left her high and dry at the party when the cops arrived.

"I thought you artsy types were supposed to have a more live-and-let-live lifestyle."

Was his tone faintly mocking or was the alcohol screwing with her judgment? "Those stories of wild artists are mainly a myth."

"So you consider yourself an artist and not a middle school teacher?"

Again his words seemed laced with a trace of superiority. "We can't all be hotshot lawyers and judges," she countered.

"You're right. It takes a particular intellect to succeed in those fields."

Beth swallowed an angry retort. Aiden couldn't help being a bit of a snob, considering he was raised by Cynthia. She rose to her feet and then quickly grabbed the table to keep from losing balance. Wine had never affected her so quickly before. Drinking on an empty stomach didn't agree with her. "Thanks for bringing the wine, Aiden, but I think I need to take a little nap before Sammy comes back."

Aiden chuckled. "It's catching up to you, huh?"

No point denying it. "Yes." She gestured to the door. "We'll talk later. Congratulations again on your firm's success."

"This wasn't much of a celebration. Tell you what, let's you and me go on over to the Polaris. Sammy can join us when he finishes business."

"I don't feel like going out."

"You need food," he said firmly. "How long since you've eaten?"

She thought through the fog clouding her mind. "Not since a late breakfast."

"There you go then. The Polaris is only a few blocks away. You can walk off the effect of the drink and eat dinner. You don't want Sammy to see you sloppy drunk, do you? What would he think?"

"I suppose you have a point," she said with a longing glance at the bed.

Aiden took her arm, leading her to the door. "I'll get a taxi. Trust me, going out to eat is just what you need."

With a sigh, she looked around for her purse, then spotted it on the nightstand. "Let me get my purse."

"No need. This is my treat."

"If you're sure—"

"Least I can do after all you've done for me. I couldn't ask for a better sister. It was my lucky day when Mom married your dad."

Aiden unlocked the door and she stumbled into the hallway. The floor felt uneven and her stomach rumbled. "I feel sick. Maybe I better—"

"No." His grip on her arm seemed to tighten.

"But—"

Instead of slowing down to accommodate her wobbly feet, Aiden quickened his pace and they walked past the elevators.

Beth frowned and tried to sort what was happening. "Why aren't we getting on the elevator?"

"We'll take the stairs."

"But why?"

"You need to walk, sis. You're right—that wine went straight to your head. Besides, I can't be seen with you stumbling around in public. What if I ran into an important client or a colleague?"

Heat rose in her cheeks. "Going out was your idea." She tried to jerk her arm free, but Aiden tightened his grip even more.

"Don't be so sensitive," he chided. "I'm doing this for you, not me."

They reached the end of the hallway. Beth dug in her feet at the exit stairwell door. "I've changed my mind."

He tugged at her elbow, his jaw set stubbornly. "Too late for that."

Chapter Thirteen

Sammy entered the interrogation room, noting that it looked almost identical to the one in Elmore County. He suspected every such room at any police station looked much the same—windowless, dreary colors, cheap linoleum floors and no furniture except for a table and couple of metal chairs.

Dorsey Lambert sat slumped in a chair, scowling at the gouged surface of the table. He didn't raise his head when Sammy entered. A uniformed cop rose and nodded as he exited the room. "He's all yours."

Sammy took a seat across from Lambert, who stubbornly refused to face him. He waited, sweating him out. A full minute rolled by before the suspect met his gaze. "Who are you supposed to be?" he demanded, evidently expecting to see someone in a cop uniform or a detective with a suit sporting a badge.

"You don't remember me? I chased you a

good three or four blocks when you bolted from your mom's home."

Recognition sparked in Lambert's unnaturally intense blue eyes. He scrubbed at his jaw, speckled with auburn stubble. The man was skinny and, as Sammy recalled, rather on the short side. But he carried himself like a mean yard dog itching for a fight and no doubt he could probably hold his own with most men twice his size. Sammy tried to think back on the height of the pipe bomb suspect who'd run away. Could there have been a third person there that night that they didn't know about? But Sammy couldn't recall anything concrete about the suspect that had tossed the bomb; it had been too dark and too brief an encounter to hazard a guess on the man's size.

"Are you the reason I'm here?" Lambert groused, lazing back in his chair. "Whatcha want with me?"

"You know why."

"No, I don't."

"Haven't you spoken with your mother?"

Lambert suddenly leaned forward and practically growled. "Leave Momma and my kin outta this."

Interesting to note the suspect felt such loyalty. "So it's okay for you and your family to terrorize a woman but then not man up when the law finally catches up to you?"

"Man up? That what you call snitching on your own family? 'Cause that ain't happening."

"I'm not here to debate semantics with you." At Lambert's blank look, he leveled him with a grim smile. "Let me put it another way. Either you cooperate, or I'll be questioning your mother every day until you confess."

Lambert sprang to his feet, chest puffed out. Sammy also rose and stared him down, daring the man to strike.

The door opened. "Need any backup?" a uniformed cop asked.

Dorsey's eyes darted nervously; he knew he was trapped.

"That's okay. I think we're ready to have a civilized conversation now, aren't we, Lambert?"

Dorsey didn't respond but slumped back down in his chair. Sammy also took a seat and tried a new tactic. "Two cousins of yours—Abbie Fenton and Marty Upshaw—are already dead. Do you really want more lives wasted? Let's end this. Right here, right now."

Dorsey's mouth twisted. "End it? You mean arrest me for only trying to get what's due me." His voice oozed with bitterness. "Ain't that always the way, though? Rich man gets away with everything while people like me and my family are the ones who suffer."

Sammy picked up on his earlier statement. "What do you mean by trying to get what you're due?"

"Judge Wynngate was dirty. Everyone knew it. With the right amount of money, you could buy an innocent verdict or get your jail time cut in half."

"Why should I believe you?"

"Why would I lie about it? I paid fifty thousand bucks and what did that bastard do for me?"

Sammy stared back at him impassively, waiting for Lambert to continue. Dorsey slammed his hand on the table. "Nothing! He did nothing. Wynngate took my money and then gave me the maximum sentence possible. All I wanted was to get my money back. That kind of money don't mean nothing to some rich bitch like his daughter. She should give it back to me."

Sammy grabbed a fistful of Lambert's flannel shirt. "Don't you dare call her that." Conscious he was being watched, Sammy reluctantly let go. "Beth Wynngate has nothing to do with her father's so-called crimes."

"Yeah, but she inherited his dirty money, now, didn't she? I seen it in the papers after he died. She got nearly all of it. All I ask is that she give back what's rightfully due me and my family. Scraping together that money was a real hardship on us. And while I was in prison, I couldn't hold down a job and help out my momma. Without my paycheck, she lives off a measly government check that don't cover all she needs."

Regular paycheck? Dorsey Lambert was a known drug dealer, not a stalwart employee earning an honest income, but Sammy let that go for now.

"I fail to see how killing Beth Wynngate is going to get your money returned to you."

Dorsey's eyes widened, and his jaw slackened. "Kill her? Ain't nobody trying to kill her."

"Don't lie to me! Why else were Marty and Abbie out there when the cabin exploded?"

Confusion clouded his eyes. "What cabin explosion?"

Sammy narrowed his eyes at him. Dorsey appeared surprised, but ex-cons were often good actors. His department hadn't reported the arson crime to the newspapers so the few Lavender Mountain locals who knew the fire department had been called out didn't know what had caused the fire.

"I know about the high-speed chase. Weren't

no mention in the papers about a cabin exploding. We ain't got nothing to do with that."

"You saying your cousin Marty didn't have anything to do with it?"

"No, sir." Some of Dorsey's defiant bravado faded. "I admit they were out there keeping watch on Wynngate. I told them to wait for an opportunity when she was alone and then lean on her again about the money. Last time I talked to them, they'd followed y'all out to the cabin. Figured you'd return to work the next day and Wynngate would be alone at the cabin. The perfect opportunity to squeeze her for the money."

Sammy's blood chilled at the thought of Beth being alone in the woods and "squeezed" for money. "Let's back everything up a minute. Tell me more about your claim of paying off Judge Wynngate."

Dorsey shrugged. "Everybody knew he could be bought."

"You got any proof you paid him this money?"

"No," he admitted, his voice souring again. "I didn't pay him directly. I paid one of his collectors. Cash. Just as I was told to do."

"Who took your money?"

A cagey look came over his face. "Don't know his name."

"You're lying. You expect me to believe you paid a stranger fifty thousand in cash?" Dorsey wasn't the sharpest tool in the shed, but he did appear to have some street smarts.

"I did. I swear it's true. Some buddies of mine got time shaved off their sentences doin' the same thing."

"And how do you know this collector didn't just pocket the money and never forwarded it to the judge?"

"He paid him," Dorsey insisted. "Just my bad luck that federal heat was coming down on the judge not long after he took my money. The middleman told me I'd have to wait it out a few months. If Wynngate gave me a light sentence, it could be viewed in a negative light for the judge. The feds were looking for a pattern. Guy told me that when the heat died down, the judge would lighten my sentence on appeal."

First thing he needed to check was Lambert's claim of a federal investigation on the judge. He'd see if Harlan could use his contacts to find out unofficially. That should prove much faster than a formal inquiry.

Dorsey kicked at the empty chair beside him in disgust. "Then the bastard up and dies on me. Can you believe that crap? All that money wasted."

"Forget about the money. It's gone and you'll never get it back. You've already done your time. It's over. Think of the future. Now you're looking at a bigger mess. Attempted murder."

Dorsey threw up his hands, eyes wide with panic. "I wasn't anywhere near that cabin. I've been here in Atlanta at my mom's house. Didn't even know about the explosion until you told me five minutes ago."

"Yet you readily admit you had family members there that night, working for you."

"They didn't do it! I know them. They wouldn't kill nobody."

"Why should I believe a word you're telling me?"

"Ask around. Check with the feds about my story. Look, man, all I wanted was my money back. I ain't never killed anybody and don't plan on starting now."

Sammy steepled his fingers and regarded Dorsey's pleading eyes. "So you say. But greed and revenge are powerful motives for murder. I'd say both of those factors are at play in your head."

"I didn't do it!" He kicked at the chair again.

"If you're not guilty we'll find out soon enough. But your admission about involving your cousins in a scheme to extort money from Beth Wynngate is pretty damning. It places them right at the scene of the crime."

"That don't prove nothing. You can't keep me here."

"Of course we can. You've technically broken parole."

Dorsey squeezed his eyes shut and crinkled his nose, evidently regretting his words. He crossed his arms over his chest. "I want a lawyer."

Of course he did. Sammy nodded and rose. "Don't even think about asking anyone else in your family to come after Beth Wynngate. If you do, I'll make sure you're so old by the next time you get out of prison that you'll go directly into a nursing home to live out whatever's left of your sorry life."

"I ain't messin' with her no more. You have my word," Dorsey said, surprising him. Then again, a man would say anything to avoid returning to prison.

As though reading his mind, Dorsey spoke once more. "Like you said, the past is the past. My money's gone. Best I can hope for now is to live out my days in peace. Try to be an honest man."

Sammy walked to the door, but Dorsey hadn't finished speaking his mind.

"Sounds like someone's trying to kill that girl, but it ain't me."

THE ATLANTA TRAFFIC was heavy. Sammy kept hitting redial on his phone, but Beth didn't answer. With every failed ring, his unease grew.

Surely she hadn't already gone out on the town on her own. And not while there were so many unanswered questions. Hell, they still bore the scars from last night's attempt on her life. Impatiently, he began weaving his way through the clogged lanes as fast as possible. At the hotel, he left the Jeep parked at the main entrance. "Back in a moment," he told the startled valet drivers.

Sammy raced through the lobby and entered the elevator, punching the button for the thirty-third floor. When the elevator door opened, he pushed through and scanned the hallway. To his left, he took in the sight of a man and a woman about to enter the exit stairwell. Relief washed over him.

"Where are y'all going?" he called out to Aiden and Beth, rushing over to them. "I've been trying to call."

Something was off. Beth looked disgruntled and wobbly all at once. Aiden's eyes flashed with an annoyance that was replaced so quickly with his usual effervescent charm that Sammy wondered if he'd seen it in the first place. And after the scene at his condo earlier, why the hell had he come around? That must account for the frustration in Beth's eyes. She was still upset over his remarks a few hours ago.

"We were going to go out for a drink at the

Polaris, but Beth changed her mind," Aiden said smoothly. "She decided to wait for your return. Tells me you're planning a celebration this evening."

Sammy glanced at Beth. She placed a hand on her forehead and shot him a rueful smile. "I might have to take a rain check on the celebration dinner. Aiden brought over some merlot and it's hit my system like a ton of bricks."

Aiden chuckled. "Seems my sister can't hold her liquor."

That didn't sound like Beth to overdrink. It seemed out of character. "The celebration can wait," he said.

"Sounds good. Guess I'll head on back home." Aiden extended a hand to Sammy. "We'll do it another night?"

"Sure. I'll call you."

"Great. Catch you later." Aiden raised an arm at the stairwell door. "Guess I'll take the stairs and burn some calories."

Beth started back toward their room and stumbled. He grabbed her elbow to keep her from falling. "Easy now."

She drew a deep breath. "Thanks. I can't believe how dizzy I am."

"If you're dizzy, why in hell were y'all going to take the stairs instead of the elevator?"

She grimaced. "Seems that in my present

condition, Aiden was afraid I'd embarrass him in the lobby."

"Then he shouldn't have taken you out. Period. Besides, you'd have been in public with him anyway at the Polaris."

Beth shook her head, as if to clear mental cobwebs. "Right. Who knows what he was thinking? I love my brother, but sometimes he befuddles me."

"What was he doing here? Apologizing again?"

"Yep. Showed up with a bottle of merlot and a hangdog expression." She gave a soft chuckle. "I can't stay angry with him when he pulls that."

For the second time that day, unease prickled down his back and he slowed his steps. Beth cocked her head to the side and smiled. "What's the matter? Somebody step on your grave?"

He tamped down the apprehension. Beth was here with him, a little tipsy, but they were both intact. A small miracle considering last night's attack. This was still a cause for celebration. Maybe he should wait until tomorrow to tell her of Dorsey's claims. After all, the ex-con could be lying. And she'd been so angry at him when the intruder had entered her house and he'd asked if the judge might have had some secret. He and Harlan would investigate his allegations about her father. If they were true, then Beth would be the first person he told.

Inside their room, he led her to the bed and propped her up with pillows. "I'll call room service and we'll have dinner by candlelight right here. No need to go out."

"Perfect," she agreed with a grin. "Just don't order celebratory champagne. I'm not up for it."

Neither was he, matter of fact. Thanks to Dorsey Lambert. A small corner of his mind remained disquieted. The case still didn't feel over.

Not yet.

Chapter Fourteen

Beth glowed with contentment as she gazed around her Falling Rock home. In only two days, Cynthia had arrived and taken charge of the holiday decorations. A twelve-foot-high balsam fir in the den was lit with twinkling lights and the fireplace mantel decorated with fresh garland and cinnamon-scented pine cones. In every room, even the bathrooms, Cynthia had set out scented candles and holiday figurines. Beth had to hand it to her stepmother; she was a whiz at creating a warm, cozy atmosphere at Christmas, right down to the aroma of freshly baked gingerbread and cookies. Her nesting instincts at this time of year contrasted with her usual social activities of superficial cocktail parties.

The oven alarm dinged. "Pull out that pan for me, hon," Cynthia called out, elbow-deep in a new batch of cookie dough.

Beth retrieved the lightly browned chocolate

chip cookies and set them on the cooling rack. Much as she was enjoying the domestic bonding with Cynthia, a small part of her remained hurt that she'd cut out on Beth last week after the first sign of trouble. Of course, she hadn't expected Cynthia to stay in the house, but it rankled that her stepmother hadn't even offered to have her as a guest at her Atlanta home until the danger had passed.

At least she was thankful that the threat had been removed. Nothing suspicious had happened since Dorsey Lambert's arrest. Even though he'd been released yesterday, Beth hadn't received even a hang-up call or any hint she was being followed. The only matter casting a tinge of sadness today was the thought of returning to Boston next week. How much did Sammy care that she'd be leaving? They'd been almost inseparable the last few days. When he wasn't at work, he spent all his free time with her. The thought of their returning to their normal lives living hundreds of miles apart made her heart pinch.

As though she'd conjured Sammy from sheer willpower, his Jeep pulled into the circular driveway.

"You should fill a tin with cookies for him," Cynthia suggested. Beth shook her head in bemusement. Since arriving, Cynthia had been friendly with Sammy instead of acting formal and vaguely condescending. Beth wasn't naive enough to think she actually approved of her choice in boyfriends, but her stepmother probably figured there was no harm in their temporary relationship. Beth would be leaving soon enough.

She strode to the front door and flung it open, determined to enjoy whatever time was left with Sammy.

He didn't return her welcoming smile.

Now what? "Is it Lambert? Has he done something?" she asked, holding the door open.

He entered, glancing into the kitchen where Cynthia hummed along with a Christmas carol as she continued baking. "We need to talk. Somewhere private."

Must be serious. "Downstairs, then."

Only when they were seated in the recreation room did he lean forward and speak. "When I interviewed Lambert earlier this week he claimed that he paid a middleman to have your father reduce his drug sentence."

"That's absurd," she scoffed, raising her voice. "What a piece of—"

"Don't shoot the messenger."

Beth gritted her teeth. "Go on. What else did he lie about?"

"As I was saying, Lambert claimed to have

paid fifty thousand dollars for your father to lighten his sentence. He started harassing you in the hopes of getting his money back. He had two family members, he wouldn't name names, search your father's study that night, seeking proof of payment."

"What good would that do? Even if there was, it's not like he could enter a store and show a receipt to return merchandise and get his money returned."

"I'm sure he believed you'd do anything to protect your father's reputation, including paying him off."

"Blackmail," she said grimly. "Not that I would ever have agreed to such a thing."

"No doubt Lambert wouldn't be satisfied with merely getting his money back."

"He'd start asking for interest, then payment for the pain and suffering of being incarcerated. It would never end." She observed Sammy's set face more closely. "But Lambert's claim is nothing new. What else did he say?"

"That federal authorities were investigating your dad several months before he died."

Beth couldn't speak right away, and she bit the inside of her mouth to stop the involuntary tremble of her lips. "You wouldn't be telling me this if you didn't think it was true."

He nodded. "I checked it out. Your father was

under investigation after numerous allegations that he accepted bribes."

"Go on," she whispered at his pause, expecting the worst.

"There appeared to be some validity to the claims, but they dropped the investigation upon his death."

"I see." She pictured the last time she'd seen her father, in the hospital ICU unit after triple bypass surgery. Had the stress of an investigation contributed to his heart attack? Sammy took her hand and gave it a squeeze.

"But it's possible Dad was innocent," she insisted. "I mean, they didn't actually declare him guilty of any crime."

"Anything's possible."

Beth blinked back tears. Sammy was just being kind. More than likely, her dad had been involved in shady business. He drew a nice salary as a federal judge, but they'd enjoyed a very luxurious lifestyle—expensive schools, oversea travels, gorgeous homes. Perhaps, in hindsight, that had been a bit of a stretch based on his salary. But she'd always attributed the wealth to his smart investments and side businesses.

With a sinking heart, she remembered one odd fact that had struck her after Dad died and the will had been probated. He'd owned several companies, but four months prior to his death, he'd liquidated them all. At the time, she'd wondered if he'd done so because he had a premonition of his deteriorating health and wanted to simplify his financial affairs.

"Does Cynthia know about that investigation?" she asked.

"You know her better than I do. What do you think?"

Beth considered her own question. She hadn't been living nearby to see them regularly while all this had been going on, but she didn't recall anything that would lead her to believe Cynthia was aware of possible impending doom. There had been no whispered conversations, or sudden talks of Dad retiring early. Nothing to indicate they were anything but settled and happy in their comfortable life.

"I don't think Cynthia knows anything," she said slowly.

"I don't know what?"

They both whipped their heads around. Cynthia stood halfway down the carpeted stairs, an oven mitt in one hand and a tray of cookies in the other.

Beth stood and ran a hand through her hair. "I didn't hear you coming."

"Obviously." Her stepmother gazed back and forth between them. "What's going on?"

Sammy shot her a sideways look that said, "This is up to you."

"Maybe I should tell her. I mean, if Lambert came after me for money, she might be in danger, too."

"Danger?" Cynthia slowly made her way down the steps and laid the cookies on a coffee table. "Tell me what's going on. I thought Lambert had been arrested."

"He's already been released. You better sit down for this." Beth gestured toward the couch and they sat, Sammy across from them. "You know Sammy interviewed Dorsey Lambert earlier this week and he claimed to have paid Dad for a lighter sentence."

Cynthia's lips pressed together for an instant. Her face reddened, and she removed the mitt from her hand, smacking it down on the sofa. "He's nothing but a liar. Surely you don't believe him, do you?"

Sammy cleared his throat. "Actually, there was an ongoing federal investigation prior to your husband's death. Were you aware of that?"

Cynthia's mouth parted in astonishment. "Investigation? Are you sure?"

"Yes, ma'am. I personally spoke with the federal officer overseeing it."

"Why, I—I don't know what to say. Edward

never said a word to me." Cynthia cast her a bewildered glance. "Beth?"

"He didn't say anything to me, either."

Cynthia leaped to her feet. "I refuse to believe any of this nonsense. Lambert and other convicts are just scumbags. The dregs of society. They'll say anything to cause trouble."

Sammy pulled out his cell phone. "Be that as it may, take a look at this latest mug shot of Dorsey Lambert. Wouldn't hurt for you to be aware of his appearance, so you can be on the lookout."

Cynthia gave it a quick glance, her lips curled in a sneer. "He looks thoroughly disreputable. I can't believe you'd entertain him, or others like him, for one minute. Do you really think my husband could have done such a despicable thing?

Sammy tucked the cell phone back in his pocket. "I don't know, ma'am. We might never know the full truth given his untimely death."

"I know the truth. You didn't know him like I did. Like *we* knew him. How dare you come in my home and besmirch Edward's name?"

"Sammy's only doing his job," Beth said, gently patting Cynthia's arm. "He's not accusing Dad. He came here to warn us."

"Fine. I've been warned." Cynthia stood and lifted her chin at Sammy. "Now I want you to leave my house. And Christmas Eve dinner tomorrow night? Forget it."

Beth's face flamed with heat. It was one thing for her stepmother to assume that superior air with her, but she wouldn't tolerate it being aimed at someone she cared about. Sammy started to rise, apparently unruffled at Cynthia's outburst, but Beth gestured for him to stay seated.

"Actually, Cynthia, if you want to get technical about it, this is my house. Dad left this place to me and the Atlanta home to you. So Sammy is staying and he's having dinner with us tomorrow, too."

Cynthia's haughty mien crumbled in an instant. She opened her mouth to speak, and then clamped it shut. Tears pooled in her eyes.

Damn. She hadn't meant to hurt her feelings; she'd only wanted to stop her from trying to order Sammy around. Cynthia spun on her heel and headed to the stairs.

"Wait a minute, I'm sorry," Beth began. But Cynthia held up a palm, warding off her apology. She disappeared from sight, and seconds later the door slammed shut behind her.

Sammy gave a low whistle. "Didn't mean to cause trouble for you. Is it always this tense between the two of you?"

"Without Dad as a buffer—yes. It's not like

we have a whole lot in common. Things are better when Aiden's around. He keeps the conversation going and smooths out any friction. Thank heavens he's coming in tomorrow and staying over the weekend."

"You know, you're always welcome to spend the holiday with my family," he offered. "It's a large, boisterous household when we all get together. There's my uncle and his bunch, and several cousins and their kids. Always plenty of commotion and conversation," Sammy said with a grin. "It may make you want to come running back here for a little peace and quiet."

No, what it sounded like was a loving family who enjoyed getting together. Would they really appreciate an outsider horning in on their celebration? "I'm already spending Christmas Day with you at your dad's. Don't want to overstay my welcome."

"You won't be." He hugged her and planted a quick kiss on her forehead. She rested the side of her face against the crisp cotton fabric of his uniform shirt, inhaling the clean linen smell mixed with a hint of a leathery aftershave. Her dismay at Cynthia's outburst seeped out of her body. She'd work things out with her stepmother. They always had before. She could suck it up a few more days until Cynthia returned to Atlanta and she to Boston.

Boston.

She pulled Sammy to her a little tighter, wanting to savor every possible moment they were together.

"You okay?" he asked in a husky voice that sent shivers—the good kind—down her back.

Beth pasted on a bright smile. "Fine. Guess you need to get back to work, huh?"

He held her shoulders, gazing deep into her eyes. "I have a few things to check on, but if you need me, I'm all yours."

"No, you should go. I'll talk to Cynthia now."

It took a few minutes to reassure him all was well, but at last she waved at him from the doorway as he drove off. Cynthia was nowhere in sight. Beth walked through the kitchen, noting that the oven had been turned off and all the baking supplies put away. Cynthia wasn't in the dining room or den, either. Had she been so upset that she'd packed up her things and left?

She opened the door and peeked into the garage. Cynthia's silver Town Car was still there. Perhaps she'd retired to her bedroom, unwilling to face her. She should apologize for sounding so harsh. Beneath her somewhat icy exterior, Cynthia was an emotional woman.

As she passed by the French doors in the den, a movement from outside froze her midstride.

A camo-colored ATV motored by the edge of the woods. On her property.

Anger infused her body and without thinking, she hurried to the door and opened it. "Hey," she called out. "What are you doing?"

The driver braked and stared at her for an instant. He was tall and wore a large brown parka. A black ski cap covered his head, but strings of long red hair peeked out.

Not Dorsey, but he could definitely be a member of the Lambert clan. Her breath caught, and she hastily stepped back inside. In a burst of engine pedal-hitting-metal noise, the man drove the ATV into the woods and out of sight.

But not out of mind. Beth slammed the door shut and locked it, remembering how recently two men had broken into her home and destroyed the previous door. She placed a hand on her heart, feeling it pound inside her rib cage. Should she call Sammy? Grab Cynthia and insist they leave at once and spend the holidays in Atlanta?

In the end, she did neither. *Probably only a hunter scouting locations*, she told herself. *Or somebody just bored and out for a ride.* It wouldn't be the first time they'd seen people along the tree line of Blood Mountain. ATV riding was a popular activity in the area.

Beth rubbed her arms, relieved she wasn't

alone in the house. There was safety in numbers. Maybe she should give Aiden a call and see if he could come earlier than originally planned. It would soothe Cynthia and lighten the mood. Impulsively, she lifted the receiver of the landline to call him.

"I miss you so much, baby. I hate we're so far apart."

Oops. Cynthia was already on the line. She must have wanted Aiden to come home earlier, as well. Beth started to hang up the phone when an unfamiliar, deep voice spoke.

"Ditch the family. It's been a year. Bad enough we had to sneak around when your husband was alive. But now?"

Surprise rooted Beth to the spot, hand gripped on the phone that she held to an ear. Who the hell was this man? Cynthia was a cheater. Had Dad discovered this before he died?

"Just a little longer, sweetheart," her stepmother murmured. "If we're seen together too soon, people might start to wonder how long we've been a thing."

"I don't give a damn what people think and neither—"

"And from there, some might even speculate how convenient it was for us that Edward died while I was having an affair. After all, I did end up collecting some of his money in the will."

Beth held her breath and an ominous chill ghosted across her flesh. She could hardly reconcile the grief-stricken Cynthia at her father's funeral with this woman speaking so casually to her lover about the will. She hoped Dad had never suspected. That until the very end he'd been happily married and blissfully ignorant of his wife's deceit.

"You should have gotten *all* the money," the mystery man groused.

Cynthia laughed. A high-pitched artificial sound that grated on Beth's ears. "I couldn't agree more. But what's done is done. I had no idea I wouldn't collect everything. If I'd known seven months earlier that Edward would leave Beth most of his estate, then I would have done things differently."

Things? What things? What had her step-mother done?

"Did you hear something on the line?" Cynthia asked sharply.

Beth bit her lip and wildly glanced around the room. If she hung up now, they'd definitely hear a click as the call disconnected. She raised a shaky hand to her mouth to stifle any betraying gasp.

"Nope. You're paranoid," the man said, barking out a small chuckle. "Always worried others will discover your little secrets. Why the hell did you call me on the landline anyway?"

"I forgot to charge my cell phone battery last night. Anyway, I should get off the phone, just to be safe. I'll call you later tonight."

"Come home soon," he said.

The line went dead. Beth immediately placed the phone back on the receiver. *That's what you get when you eavesdrop on people*, she heard her father's reproving voice scold in her mind. *It will never be anything good.* But it wasn't like she'd meant to listen in on a private conversation. Not really. Not until the conversation had taken such a dark, twisty path. Then she'd been hooked and there was no going back.

The scent of chocolate and caramelized sugar suddenly turned cloyingly sweet. The air felt oppressively hot and humid from all the residual heat still radiating from the oven.

She had to get out of there. She couldn't face Cynthia. Not now. Not until she'd worked out everything she'd overheard. Beth scrambled through a kitchen drawer, searching for pen and paper. She'd leave Cynthia a note that she'd gone out for a bit.

A door screeched open upstairs. Cynthia was coming.

Floorboards creaked, and footsteps started

down the hallway, then onto the stairs leading
to the den. Strange to think of all the times
she'd ever spent with Cynthia and now the
idea of being alone with her filled her with
disgust and anxiety. Beth desperately snatched
her purse from the counter and stole a quick
glance up.

Cynthia stood at the top of the stairs, looking cool and composed again, a slight smile
curving her lips. As though she hadn't stormed
out of the recreation room ten minutes ago. As
though she hadn't been on the phone with the
lover she'd been cheating with while married.
As though she bore no ill feelings for her stepdaughter.

A lie. Everything about her was a lie.

Beth rushed to the foyer and pulled on a coat.

"Where are you going?" Cynthia asked.

"Out." Beth didn't dare glance her way,
afraid her emotions would be written all over
her face.

"Listen, don't go. I want to apologize for losing my temper. Of course, Sammy was only
doing his job. He's always welcome here."

A jolt of irritation pricked through Beth's
nervousness. How many times did she have
to remind Cynthia this was *her* home, not her
stepmother's. And it was *her* decision who
came and went.

"Good to know," Beth commented wryly.

"You're still upset."

"Of course I am." Beth unlocked the dead bolt and buttoned her coat. "I need to run to the store. Be back later."

Cynthia reached her and ran a hand through Beth's errant locks. It took all of her willpower not to cringe from the woman's touch.

"Okay. I hope you realize I was only upset because of the slur to your father's name."

As if you care, Beth wanted to scream. Had Cynthia ever really loved her father? Or had it always been about the money from day one? Another one of those mysteries she'd probably never learn the answer to.

Without responding, Beth hurried out the door and into the cool, bracing air. After the stifling hot kitchen, the fresh winter breeze was as refreshing as a gulp of iced tea in the heat of a Georgia summer. She felt Cynthia's assessing eyes upon her as she opened the rental car door and slipped inside. Thank goodness Lilah had been so thoughtful to arrange a rental for her to use temporarily.

Her mind swirled, recalling every word of the overheard conversation.

Always worried others will discover your little secrets…

How convenient it was for us that Edward died while I was having an affair...

If I'd known seven months earlier that he'd leave Beth half of his estate, then I would have done things differently.

The more she ruminated, the more sinister the implications grew. Could Cynthia have played a part in her father's death? Perhaps his heart attack was brought on by the shock of discovering her affair. She had to concede that if that were the case, his heart probably wasn't in good condition to begin with.

How could Cynthia have betrayed him like this? Dad had rescued her from a minimum-wage job as a nurse's aide where she'd struggled to make ends meet for herself and her young son, Aiden. Dad had given her everything—a beautiful home, a first-class education for her son, a lifestyle that included travel and security—and all his love and loyalty.

The security guard at the gate waved at her as she passed through. Not that he'd done much good when her house had been broken into the first time. It was way too easy to access the Falling Rock houses via the woods at the back of the subdivision.

Beth shook her head as she left the gated community. What was she doing driving out of her own neighborhood? Instead of fleeing, she should have booted Cynthia out of the house. It had been such a shock to learn of her deceit that her first instinct had been to get away until she was more in control of her feelings. To hell with that. Next opportunity to turn around, she'd take it.

She started down the narrow mountain road and tapped the brakes as she came to the first bend. Nothing. She pressed her foot down until the pedal jammed against the floorboard. The car only gathered speed as it began its descent.

Panic bore down her, squeezing her chest with dread and fear. The car sped faster with every turn. To keep from going over the edge of the mountain, she had to drive in the middle of the road. If someone else came around a curve, they were both toast.

Be calm. Think.

She was already over halfway down. An S curve loomed about fifty feet ahead—bad news—but the good news was that the side of the road broadened at the curve's end. If she could just manage this last curve, she could pull over onto flat land and hope that the car would eventually stop in the wide plain before she crashed into a tree.

If, if, if.

But there was no time to speculate on her chance of survival. She desperately jerked one way on the steering wheel, then the opposite, trying to keep the vehicle from either veering off the mountain or crashing against its rocky side.

This was it. The last bend in the curve. She only had seconds to exit off the road and into flat terrain. Beth yanked at the steering wheel and the car bounced as it traversed the bumpy field. But at least she was losing speed and not endangering anyone else's life. Too soon, the open field ended, and trees jutted the landscape. She was headed straight on to a collision with a copse of pine trees.

Should she open the door and try to roll away from the car's path? Or would she risk injury by staying in the car and jerking the wheel in time to either avoid the tree or have it only hit the rear?

Beth opted to remain in the car. She gripped the steering wheel and twisted it. Her muscles tensed, anticipating impact.

Bang!

Metal crashed against bark and the car fishtailed. She held on to the steering wheel, praying that the force of the collision didn't send her body flying through the front window. Her torso strained against the seat belt. An explosion of sound and force slammed into her consciousness, so powerful her teeth rattled.

The world went white. It was as though she'd been thrown into a blinding snowstorm, so thick that it smothered, choking out the rest of the universe. Only this snow scalded. She breathed in hot fumes of dust. Beth struggled to understand what was happening.

The ivory veil abruptly dropped. She blinked. Dazedly, she glanced down and noted a deflated bag and broken sunglasses on her lap. How did they get there? Pale yellow smoke curled up from the bag and a film of dust coated the dashboard.

The dashboard…she was seated in an unmoving car. How strange. She looked out the shattered window and took in the snowy field and green pines. Where was she? Beth pulled at the door handle, but it was jammed shut. She was trapped.

Yet the idea didn't fill her with alarm. The observation merely floated through her mind like a cloud on a windy day. Again, she glanced down and saw her purse on the passenger floorboard, its contents spilled. The black screen of the cell phone seemed to blink at her as it caught a gleam of sunlight.

She undid her seat belt and leaned over to collect it, wincing as her banged-up muscles protested the movement. The solid weight of it in her palm brought her slowly back into focus, grounding her to the present reality. She'd driven off the road and hit a tree.

The moment of blankness and scalding heat she'd felt was from where the deployed airbag had punched her upper torso. In the dashboard mirror she saw several abrasions to her face and chest.

But she was alive.

And then she remembered the suddenly defective brakes. The terrifying sensation of being at the mercy of four tons of metal careening down a mountain. Had it been a freak accident or had someone tampered with them? Someone who wanted her dead. Someone named Dorsey Lambert.

Fear sharpened her dull senses and she spun her head left to right, searching for anyone lying in wait. To her immense relief, she appeared to be utterly alone. Beth turned off the sputtering engine and punched in Sammy's number.

He answered almost immediately, and she filled him in on the situation.

"I'll be right there," he assured her. "I'll send an ambulance, too. Just to make sure you're really okay."

Beth huddled deeper into her coat, the outside chill beginning to seep inside the idle, smashed car.

Chapter Fifteen

"Here you go." Charlotte placed a Dixie Diner to-go bag on his desk. Sammy's stomach grumbled at the aroma of fried chicken and cornbread, reminding him that he'd missed lunch. He pushed aside paperwork and pulled out the container.

"Jeb says the brake lines were definitely cut," Charlotte said, plopping down on the chair beside him and idly rubbing her belly. "Is that enough to see if the Atlanta PD can pick up Dorsey Lambert again for questioning?"

"Already called them. Lambert's pulled another disappearing act."

She rolled her eyes. "Of course he did."

Sammy bit into a chicken wing, suddenly ravenous. "I want you to see something," he said as he dug into his meal. He pushed the computer monitor toward Charlotte. "Click on that video."

She watched the three-minute video with

a puzzled frown. "So who are these people? What's going down here?"

"It's Aiden Wynngate, Beth's stepbrother. He's talking to Tommy Raden, a well-known Atlanta criminal with suspected ties to the mafia."

Charlotte peered more closely and leaned forward as though trying to pick out the men's conversation from the background noise of automobiles. "No better audio with this, I'm assuming?"

"None. Atlanta PD has been following Raden as part of a sting operation. I asked if I could review any recent video or audio of criminals suspected of bribing judges and politicians."

"To see if you could catch Lambert talking to one and collaborate his story?" she asked.

"Yep. Imagine my surprise to find Aiden on my screen."

"What do you suppose it means?"

He wiped his hands and swilled iced tea before answering. "Good question. I know the guy well, or I used to. We were friends growing up."

"But you aren't now?" Charlotte was always quick on the uptake.

"Not since he left for college and I went to work in this place." He shrugged. "Different worlds. We drifted apart."

She tapped the side of her jaw with her index finger, studying him as he resumed digging into the fried chicken. "Do you think he's in league with Lambert to hurt Beth? And if so, what's in it for him?"

"That's what I'm trying to figure out."

"What can I do to help?" she asked, always ready to get down to business.

"Nothing. I've fished around, trolling for the usual information. I'm waiting on some emails to come in. You go on home. If I need you, I'll call you."

"Promise?"

"Absolutely."

Charlotte slowly rose to her feet, wobbled a moment and then swiped a hand across her brow. He frowned. "You need me to call James to come pick you up? Or I could give you a ride home."

She shook her head. "I can drive myself home. See you in the morning."

He watched as she slowly made her way to the lobby, wondering if the baby had decided to make an early appearance. Wouldn't surprise him if James called in the morning announcing the arrival of a baby. It was times like this that reminded Sammy just how alone in the world he'd become over the years. One by one, all of his closest friends had gotten married and most were now raising children.

Sammy mentally shrugged off the disquieting thought. He had plenty of time to muse on his life choices later. Right now, he needed to solve this puzzle of Aiden and his contact with Raden. Aiden was a criminal attorney now, so it was possible Raden was a client. Could there be more to it than just an attorney-client relationship, though?

Could Aiden be responsible for any of the attempts on Beth's life? The question went round and round in his mind. Sammy stood and paced the office, ruminating over dark, dangerous possibilities.

At least Beth was protected for the moment. It had taken lots of persuading, but she'd agreed to spend the night with Lilah. Harlan's place was as good as a safe house. By morning, Cynthia would be ousted from the Falling Rock home and kicked back to Atlanta.

With something of a shock, he realized night had crept up on him. Most of the downtown shops were closed and under the yellow streetlamp beams. The only people out and about were a few coming and going from the diner.

His computer dinged, signaling an incoming email. He hurried back to his desk and saw he had missed several messages. He opened the first one and scanned the bank records he'd requested. Thankfully, he was able to access them because of the ongoing criminal probe of Raden. The numbers confirmed why Aiden had sought a loan from Beth. Both his personal and business accounts had bounced checks and had huge outstanding credit card balances from extravagant expenditures and high rent.

Next, Sammy turned to the message from his friend at the Elmore County Courthouse. After scrolling through pages of legalese he found the bottom line—Judge Wynngate had left seventy percent of his estate to Beth and thirty percent to his wife. It wasn't unusual to see children inherit the majority of an estate upon a person's second marriage, but Cynthia might not have viewed the terms in such a light. Perhaps she was determined to gain the rest of the inheritance she believed rightly belonged to her and not Beth? And if she was, she might have recruited her son in the effort.

He mopped his face with a hand and sighed. Beth's accidental discovery of Cynthia talking to her lover might have saved her life. His thoughts went deeper, darker. Did Cynthia have anything to do with her husband's unexpected heart attack? He made a note to check the hospital records in the morning before that office closed for the holiday and speak with the attending physician of record. Not much hope that would reveal anything, though. If there'd been any suspicion of foul play there would have been an autopsy and the sheriff's department would have been asked to investigate.

With no more avenues to explore, Sammy gazed out the window, absently tapping his pencil on the desktop. He briefly considered dropping by Harlan's place and asking Beth to spend the night with him instead. *No.* He was being selfish and paranoid. She'd looked so tired and haggard when he'd driven her there from the hospital after the wreck, Lilah's fierce nurturing mode had kicked in. She'd immediately embraced Beth and led her inside, fussing over her. Once Beth was seated, Lilah had immediately placed a pillow behind her back, pulled a blanket over her legs, and demanded Beth rest while she cooked a pot of chicken and dumplings.

For all he knew, Beth might have taken one of the prescribed pain pills and already be peacefully dozing.

No, tomorrow morning would be soon enough to see Beth and explore the possibility that the person, or persons, who wanted her dead might be the very ones closest to home.

Chapter Sixteen

After a nap and a home-cooked family meal, Beth at last felt better. Her automobile accident and the conversation she'd overheard earlier had unsettled her. Instead of being afraid, though, she was angry. Furious, actually. And she didn't want to wait until tomorrow morning to have a much-needed conversation with Cynthia. The sooner she got that woman out of her home, the better.

As she fumed over what to do, she reached out to her stepbrother, her hand clenched around her cell as she spoke.

"Did you know about this?" she asked, her voice filled with rage after she told Aiden of his mother's affair.

"Calm down, sis. I suspected something. I'm headed to the house, and maybe we should talk to her together. Find out what's really going on. We can present a united front," he suggested.

Relieved he was willing to help, Beth quickly

agreed. She'd feel more in the holiday spirit if she settled this with her stepmother first.

Despite Lilah objection's, Beth drove her rental car back to Falling Rock and pulled into the drive. A quick glance into the garage window showed it was empty. Had Cynthia left of her own accord, sensing that Beth was angry and onto her? So much the better.

Beth unlocked the door and entered her home, feeling a mixture of both relief and disappointment. She'd been all set to light into her stepmother and demand an explanation for her appalling behavior. But instead, she wandered aimlessly in the quiet house. The kitchen still smelled of fresh baked cookies and the Christmas tree twinkled in the gathering darkness. She marched upstairs and peeked in her stepmother's bedroom.

Cynthia had cleared out. The bed was made and the closets empty.

Beth strolled to the window and looked out over the yard. Snow blanketed the ground. The beauty of the scene made her fingers itch to capture the play of light and shadow in the twilight. Well, why not? It would give her something to do as well as quiet the unease that twisted her gut as she waited for Aiden to arrive. She'd already called him to tell him he needn't come because Cynthia was gone, but he said he was on his way and to just head to bed if she was tired. They still had things to discuss, he'd told her. Quickly, she gathered her painting materials and set to work.

Over two hours later, she'd finished the small painting and regarded it with satisfaction. Beth stood and stretched, contemplating taking another pain pill before bedtime. Ultimately, she decided plain aspirin would suffice. She'd go to bed early, as Aiden had suggested, and call Sammy first thing to tell him she'd had a change of heart and would love to spend Christmas Eve with him and his family. Mind made up, she donned pajamas and slipped into bed. It had probably been for the best she'd not had a confrontation with Cynthia this evening. Tomorrow, she'd be able to talk to her in a more civilized manner. For her father's sake, she'd be polite—but barely. As far as she was concerned, any relationship with her stepmother was officially over. And as for Aiden—the jury was still out. This past week had not brought out the best in her stepbrother. Maybe she'd always been too giving in their relationship, as well. Always the one to forgive and forget. She was glad he'd offered to confront Cynthia together, but she still wondered what his true motives were.

Beth punched at the pillow and rolled over,

struggling to find a comfortable position and quiet her mind. Again she recalled the terror of hurtling down the mountain in a car without brakes and the phone conversation she'd overheard—the little innuendos that sent spider-crawls of suspicion skittering down her spine.

Headlight beams pierced the darkness of her bedroom and the sound of a car motor interrupted the night's silence. A spark of involuntary fear paralyzed her for a moment before she pulled back the bedspread and hurried to the window. Keeping cover behind the curtain, she watched from a small slit of windowpane as the familiar dark blue sedan stopped on the driveway. Aiden sprang from the vehicle, a bottle, presumably liquor, tucked between one arm and his waist.

Too bad it hadn't been Sammy. She wasn't sure she had the energy to deal with Aiden so late in the evening. Had her brother spoken with Cynthia already? Or had her stepmother given him some sob story—that Beth had possibly overheard a conversation and misunderstood everything?

Briefly, she considered ignoring his arrival. No, she couldn't be that rude. With a sigh, Beth turned on the lamp, grabbed her robe from the foot of the bed and donned slippers. Two piercing chimes buzzed through the house as she hurried down to the main level. Already, her back and shoulders ached and protested her sudden movement. The tumble down the mountain earlier had left her body feeling slightly battered.

She flung open the door as Aiden jabbed it yet a third time.

"I'm here," she said irritably. Cold wind slapped against her body and she hugged her waist, belting the robe tighter.

Aiden pretended not to notice her cranky mood. "Where's the party?" he said with a laugh, holding up a bottle of wine. "It's not even eleven yet."

"Guess you didn't hear about my car wreck." Beth stepped aside, allowing him entrance. She'd not told him about it.

Alarm slackened his jaw and his eyes quickly scanned her body. "Oh my God! Are you okay?"

"By some miracle, I'm only sore."

"You've got scratches on your forehead. What happened? How bad was the wreck?" Aiden hung his jacket on the coat rack and followed her into the den. "And where's Mom? She never came back?"

"She never did. I thought you might have tried to reach her to find out what her side of the story was."

"No. Thought we'd talk first. Damn, sounds

like you've had a rough day all around. And I haven't helped things barging in here so late at night. Sorry, hon." Aiden gestured toward the sofa. "Sit down and put your feet up. I want to hear all about it. But first, I'll pour us a glass of bourbon."

She shook her head, then groaned at the jolt of pain in her right temple. "Better not. I took a pain pill earlier today."

"What does it matter? Just a few sips before heading to bed. It won't hurt anything."

"I'd rather not. Didn't work out for me so well last time I drank."

A dark shadow crossed his face. Did Aiden have a drinking problem? Did it make him feel better about his alcohol issue if he wasn't drinking alone? She started to give in, then stopped herself. No, it was high time she put her needs before what her family wanted and right now she didn't want a nightcap.

Aiden sighed. "Okay, okay, spoilsport. How about a cup of tea, then?"

"Great idea," she conceded. "I'll show you—"

"I know where everything is. You just relax. I'll take care of you."

That sounded wonderful. Beth sank against the couch cushions and smiled. "Not going to argue with you. I could use a little pampering after the day I've had."

"Poor kid. Be right back."

Beth glanced out the window as Aiden rumbled around in the kitchen. The night was so peaceful, so beautiful. She actually found herself looking forward to Christmas. Without Cynthia underfoot, it'd be less stressful. It would be fun meeting Sammy's family and then later she and Aiden could chill out here at home watching a couple movies and microwaving popcorn. It'd be like the old days.

Maybe Sammy wouldn't mind if Aiden had dinner with his family, as well. She'd ask him in the morning.

The kettle whistle blew and moments later Aiden appeared with a mug. "Two sugars and a splash of cream, right?"

"You got it."

He placed the mug in her hand and the heat warmed her chilled fingers. Steam spiraled upward, and she inhaled the slightly citrus aroma of the Earl Grey. It made her think of lemon orchards in the middle of winter.

"So where's your boyfriend tonight?" Aiden asked, kicking back in the recliner with a highball glass filled with bourbon and ice.

"Working late." Beth sipped her tea. *Hmm.* The taste was slightly off. Aiden must have accidently only used one packet of sugar instead of two.

"Problem?" he asked.

"Nothing," she hastened to reassure him, taking another swallow. He'd driven all the way from Atlanta and must be tired. She certainly wasn't some diva who insisted on perfection and expected others to wait on her hand and foot. "Want to have dinner tomorrow with Sammy's family? We can come back here afterward for movies and popcorn." Beth frowned. "But I guess Cynthia expects you to be with her tomorrow night?"

He lifted and dropped a shoulder. "We'll play it by ear. Right now, all I can think about is this evening. Tomorrow will take care of itself. We can work things out."

Typical Aiden. Always had been one to live in the moment. She'd wondered if law school and his new career would make him more cautious, less spontaneous. Apparently, it had not. He took a long swallow of bourbon and she studied his tight face. Despite his casual words and laissez-faire attitude, he didn't seem quite himself. Maybe he was as upset as she was about Cynthia's disloyalty. "Are you really happy in your job?"

"Couldn't be happier. Why?"

"I don't know," she said, cautiously picking her words. "You seem a bit wound up this visit. Under stress."

He snorted. "How would you even know what it feels like to be under stress? Teaching nine-year-olds how to finger-paint is hardly what anyone would call stressful. Besides, you're loaded. Born with a silver spoon, you lucky bitch."

Aiden said the words with a laugh, but they were too harsh for normal sibling teasing. Something more was at play here. She'd had no idea he resented her inheritance so much. After all, Aiden had been left a generous stipend in her father's will and she was Dad's only biological child. Not to mention some of the inherited money had come from her mother.

"Maybe you need to slow down with the drinking," she said. "Your jealousy is showing. Not a good look for you, brother. I think I'll go to bed after all. We'll talk in the morning about Cynthia. My mind's too much in a fog right now."

"No, no, you're right. I was out of line there. It's just that I've been under a lot of pressure at work trying to make a go of my new firm. Go on and finish your tea."

Beth started to rise and then shrugged. It was practically Christmas. She didn't want to argue. It wasn't like she was living with her brother, or even anywhere near him for that matter. Wasn't that what families did when thrown together for the holidays? Try to get along for the brief period of time they had with each other? She swallowed her annoyance and took a large gulp of the cooled tea. The sooner she finished, the sooner she could get to bed and end this conversation. And having Aiden in the house was comforting, what with all the break-ins and threats from Lambert and his family. In the morning, they'd decide what to do about Cynthia.

"More tea?" he asked when she set down her cup and started to rise.

"Any more caffeine and I might not sleep tonight." A rush of dizziness assaulted her as she stood, and Beth grasped the sofa arm and closed her eyes, willing the room to stop spinning.

"Feeling a bit woozy, little sister?" Aiden's voice was singsongy and chirpy. As though he found her unsteadiness amusing.

"A bit."

His hand grasped her forearm. "Good."

Good? What was that supposed to mean? Beth's eyes flew open and she stared at him.

The Aiden who stared back was a stranger. Dead eyes, a lifted chin and a curled upper lip made him appear cold and disdainful. As though…as though he hated her.

"I've got something I want you to sign." He

dragged her toward the kitchen, fingers cruelly kneading into her flesh.

Beth fought down the sudden wave of fear. This was Aiden, her brother. He could be a giant jerk, but he meant her no harm. He couldn't realize how his own strength made his grip painful. On the kitchen island, a mound of paperwork lay on the counter, a pen splayed across the top sheet. They hadn't been there before.

"Let go of me. Can't this wait until morning?"

He roughly planted her at the edge of the counter. "Do it now."

She gaped at him, startled at the mean edge in his voice. "What's wrong with you?"

"Just do as you're told. It will go easier for you."

Beth glanced down at the top sheet of the paper. The text seemed to squiggle and squirm. "I—I can't read it. What do you want me to sign?"

"Doesn't matter. Now do it."

Beth picked up the pen with shaking fingers and licked her lips. *Concentrate.* Something was very, very wrong here. She hunched over the counter and squinted her eyes. Several words and phrases leaped into coherent form. It was a legal document of some sorts: *Being of sound mind and body, bequeath to Aiden Lyle Wynngate, my legal heir, seventy-five percent of all my assets, in the event of my death.*

My death.

The full import of the words fell on Beth like a knockout punch to the gut. At least it had the effect of snapping the mental lethargy that had clouded her mind. Aiden applied a deeper, bruising pressure on her forearm. "Sign it."

"Why are you doing this?" she asked, searching his dark eyes for a spark of human warmth. But his eyes were a vacuum, a black abyss of implacable hatred and determination.

He sneered. "Isn't it obvious?"

Her fingers grasped the pen and held on to it as though it were an anchor. Her mind skittered around the source of its greatest fear and then accepted the monstrosity.

Her brother wanted to murder her for money. He'd not rushed to her side to offer comfort and counsel about Cynthia. She'd be willing to bet that he'd invented some ruse to his mother to ensure that she didn't return here today. He'd been planning on showing up all along. To get rid of her.

She'd deal with the horror of that fact later. For now, she had to keep Aiden talking, to understand every nuance of his plan. "You drugged me," she accused. "What did you put in that tea?"

"A little something to make you drowsy." He grinned, as though mentally congratulating his own cleverness.

"But…why?"

"C'mon, Beth. You aren't the brightest bulb in the pack, but you aren't totally stupid. Do I have to spell it out for you? Fine, then."

He leaned forward, his face inches from her own. The scent of bourbon on his breath made her eyes water. "I want your money. I hate people like you. So entitled. Blissfully ignorant of what it's like in the real world."

"You—you hate me?" Memories rushed past her with cyclone speed—Aiden driving her to get ice cream in the summers before she had a driver's license, Aiden teasing her about past boyfriends, Aiden who always could lighten the tension in the house with his jokes and easy manner.

He released his grip on her arm and gave a slow clap. "Now you're catching on."

"What did I ever do to you?" Beth slowly sidled away from him, hoping his attention was focused on at last spewing all the poison he harbored deep in his soul. "Dad took you and your mom in when you had nothing. He paid for your college, law school and everything in between. Doesn't that mean anything to you?"

"He died and left me nothing."

"That's not true. He left you over ten thousand dollars."

His upper lip curled. "A paltry amount. That pittance ran out four months after he died."

Beth eased another two steps back from his hulking form and eyed the knife block four feet away on the kitchen counter. If she could only divert his attention for a couple seconds, she could make a run for it and grab a knife as she raced out of the room.

"Is Cynthia in on this, too?"

"Are you kidding? She's moving on to the next sugar daddy, as you know." A sly grin flickered across his face. "Actually, she got started on that even before your dad died."

"So I learned today. Cynthia's a lot of things, but at least she isn't a murderer. Like you."

"You're defending her?" Genuine puzzlement creased his forehead.

Beth grasped at the straw that had presented itself. "Yes. No matter what else Cynthia's guilty of, she loves you, Aiden. She's always been the one to rush to your defense in every situation. Even managed to convince my own father to let me be the sacrificial goat when the cops showed up and found pot and alcohol at the party. Remember? The night you cut out and left me to shoulder all the blame."

He smirked. "Couldn't have planned it any better. I called up all my friends and acquaintances and told them to get over here. The more grass, booze and other drugs they could bring, the better. Then, I called the cops myself to tip them off and gave them the address."

"You planned that all along?"

"Of course."

Another step back. She was so close to the knives. But she dared not make a sudden grab while his attention was all on her. "Like I was saying, Cynthia loves you. If you kill me, Sammy will catch you and make sure you're put in prison for the rest of your life. What would that do to your mother to have to come visit you at a penitentiary?"

"I prefer to think of it as eliminating an obstacle, not a murder. Don't worry about her. She won't live long enough to worry about it. I can't have Mom needling me for her cut of your inheritance."

"Wh-what are you saying?"

"Mom's next."

Her gasp filled the kitchen. If Aiden was capable of killing his own mother, he was truly mad. "Think, Aiden. Please. Think this through. You're not as smart as you believe.

How's it going to look that I signed a will the day before my death? You'd be the person with the best motive to kill me. Sammy would target you in a heartbeat."

"The will's dated a year earlier, dumb ass."

"And it just happens to come to light now?"

"What better time than after someone dies? That's how wills work. Sign it and I'll safely tuck it away in a file cabinet."

There was no reasoning with a madman.

Aiden turned his back to her and toward the papers on the counter. Now was her chance—maybe her only chance. Beth leaped forward and lunged for the knife. Her right hand closed over the wooden base and she pulled one from the block. A subtle rush of air must have alerted Aiden and he wheeled around.

Beth brandished the large carving knife in front of her as she carefully backed toward the foyer. Aiden advanced, a coaxing smile on his lips.

"We both know you aren't going to use that," he said soothingly.

"Do you really want to try me?"

He frowned and shook his head. "I didn't put enough drugs in that tea."

"Mortal danger is a powerful counteractant to any sedative." Adrenal hormones were probably flooding her body. Beth kept the knife raised as she contemplated her next move. Even if she managed to reach the front door, Aiden would be on her before she could unlock it and run into the yard. Her best bet now would be to pivot, run upstairs, and then try to lock herself in one of the bedrooms. And after that? If only she could grab her cell phone to call the police—it sat, tantalizingly close, charging on the counter. But she'd have to figure out the next step once there was a locked door between her and Aiden.

The shrill ring of the landline phone buzzed through the tension between them.

Beth didn't wait to see if Aiden turned in the phone's direction. Damned if she'd just stand there and let him overtake her. Good chance he'd grab her arm before she could get a lethal cut in.

She ran. As fast and furious as she could pump her legs. She felt his breathing behind her as she climbed the stairs but couldn't risk a look around to gauge how close he was. She made it up the short flight of stairs and began running down the hardwood hallway. Aiden's footsteps pounded close behind. Oh, God, she was never going to make it. The first bedroom was on the right and she headed to it. Only three more steps…two…

Over two hundred pounds of solid flesh

knocked into her back, and she hit the floor headfirst. The knife slipped out of her grasp and clattered across the floor. Beth extended an arm, desperately stretching to reach it, but Aiden easily scooped it up first. He rolled her over onto her back and pinned her down with a knee to her stomach. The metal tip of the knife pressed into her throat.

"Let's start over. Shall we? We're going to go downstairs, you're going to sign those papers, and then we're taking a little night ride. Got it?"

Beth blinked up at the brother she'd never truly known. He didn't even appear to be all that angry, merely annoyed that she was causing so much trouble with his plans. But the absence of rage only chillingly brought home how truly crazy he must be.

"Please, Aiden," she whispered, hoping to reach some small sane part of him that might be buried in his soul.

He drew back the knife and pulled Beth to her feet. "No more nonsense now," he chided. "Can't leave a mess behind."

That was the only reason Aiden hadn't killed her yet. He didn't want to leave behind any evidence of foul play, plus he wanted her authentic signature. Once he had that, he'd drive her to a remote area in the hills and…kill her and dispose of her body.

An inexplicable calm settled over Beth as she let him lead her back into the kitchen. It almost felt as though this whole ordeal was happening to someone else and she was observing from afar. Her survival instinct had kicked in, providing a chance to try and think through her predicament and seek possible opportunities for escape.

Let him believe she'd been frightened into meek compliance. He'd be all the more startled when she seized the perfect moment to try and escape again. Wasn't that what Sammy had taught her that day in the woods? In the kitchen, Aiden sat her roughly down in a chair by the table. Without a word, he shoved the papers in front of her and handed her a pen.

She began writing her name. Should she try to signal something here? If Aiden was successful, if he killed her, shouldn't she leave behind a breadcrumb trail that would lead Sammy to her killer? *Sammy.* The surreal calm crumbled. He would be devastated. He'd find some crazy reason to blame himself for not protecting her. And if he never caught the killer? He'd probably never forgive himself. She didn't want that. Not for anyone and especially not for him.

Slowly, she wrote her first name with, hopefully, enough of an exaggerated script that might raise eyebrows at close inspection—but not so exaggerated that Aiden would notice. Would it be enough? Beth began to write her middle name, deliberating leaving out a letter to further make it look suspicious. She stole a quick peek at Aiden, who was watching her and not the writing. A mad desire arose to scribble the word *help* somewhere on the page, but she didn't dare take the chance.

"Hurry up," he demanded.

She finished her name and set down the pen. He gave it a quick glance and nodded. "Very good. I'll put these up in a good place later."

Beth swallowed hard. *Keep him talking.* "When you visited me at the W Hotel—you were going to kill me that day, weren't you? I wasn't drunk. You'd spiked my drink then, too."

Aiden scowled. "I had you right where I wanted. Didn't have you sign the will, but I would have forged your signature after. Another ten seconds and you would have plunged headfirst down the hotel stairwell. Damn Sammy for showing up when he did. What a pain in the ass."

Beth shivered, realizing how close she'd come. What did he have in mind for tonight's killing? What would his new method for murder be? Her glance strayed to the knife he'd laid on the table. *Don't dwell on that now.* "Speaking of Sammy, you underestimate him if you think he won't figure out what you've done."

"Sammy Armstrong? The same genius who believes Dorsey Lambert is behind all your accidents?"

Her eyes widened. "You mean—"

"I'm the one who cut the brake line on your car. I'm also the one who threw that pipe bomb in the cabin. Did you really think I wouldn't hunt you down there? I used that old cabin so much for partying as a teenager that it's the first place I thought of for you to run and hide. " He slammed his hand down on the table. The loud *tha-wump* echoed through the kitchen. "I can't believe it didn't kill you both."

The confession confused her. "But Dorsey's cousins were there. They ran from us."

"Oh, the Lamberts have been stalking you all right. At first, I was annoyed. Then I realized I could use that fact to my advantage. Why would anyone suspect me of killing you when Dorsey had motive and opportunity? And *that*, my dear Beth, is what Sammy is going to believe. That Dorsey or one of his kinfolks is responsible for your disappearance.

"Disappearance?" A small hope bloomed inside her chest. Maybe Aiden planned on letting her live, perhaps allowing her to assume a new identity in another country.

"Disappearance or death." He shrugged. "Depends on whether or not they find your body."

With that chilling remark, Aiden stood and grabbed his coat off the back of a kitchen chair. "And now we go for a ride."

"Where are we going?"

"You'll find out soon enough."

No way in hell she'd cooperate without a fight, like a lamb led to the slaughter. Beth jumped to her feet, grabbed a vase on the table and swung it at Aiden. The fragile glass exploded on his right temple. Blood and glass shards splattered through the air. Aiden shook his head, momentarily stunned.

Again she ran. This time she made it to the backdoor and had even managed to release the dead bolt on the lock before a sudden, searing pain exploded on her scalp. Her body was jerked back into Aiden's chest and he twisted her hair locked in his grip.

"Nice try."

She tried to remember the move Sammy had taught her when grabbed from behind, but she couldn't manage anything with the violent pull at her scalp.

He dragged her across the den and then threw her onto the sofa. Beth kicked at him, even landing a few blows to his chest and gut before he wrestled her onto her stomach. His large hands tightly gripped hers, then she felt the rough hemp of rope cut into her wrists. In short order he bound her hands, and then her ankles.

Beth rolled over onto her back and stared up where he lurked above, breathing hard and gushing blood from the head wound. Aiden swiped at the crimson streaks and winced; evidently a few glass shards had embedded into his skin.

At least I made a mess, she thought. Hopefully, enough of one that it would make her disappearance look suspicious. Because right now, it appeared that Aiden had won. She was defenseless and entirely at his mercy.

Aiden tapped a finger against his lips, studying her.

"What?" she asked breathlessly. Maybe he was rethinking his plan. Was he going to kill her right here, right now? *No, no. I'm not ready to die.* Tears poured down her cheeks, hot and salty.

"I'm debating whether or not to duct-tape your mouth shut." He shrugged and dropped his hands to his sides. "Guess there's no need to. No one will hear your screams where we're going."

"Where are you taking me?"

He wagged a finger at her, as though scolding a mischievous child. "You'll see soon enough."

"Please, Aiden…"

But he'd already turned his back, snatching an afghan from the recliner. He threw it over her, smothering her face. Beth rocked her head to and fro, frantic to fight against the sudden darkness and feeling of claustrophobia. Her warm breath was trapped underneath the knitted blanket. Was the end coming now? A death blow to her head? A gunshot wound to the heart? Strong arms gripped underneath her knees and shoulders and he carried her out the front door.

Maybe a neighbor will see him, she thought, grasping at the slight thread of hope. Unlikely given the time of night, but she prayed for it nonetheless. The door of his vehicle opened, and he flung her into the back seat as carelessly as though she were a sack of potatoes. A door slammed shut behind her. Moments later, the front door of the vehicle opened, and Aiden settled behind the wheel. Christmas music blared from the radio and he dialed down the volume, whistling along with the tune. The sedan pulled out of the circular drive.

Beth struggled and slowly managed to sit upright. The car screeched to an abrupt halt. Aiden threw back his head and laughed. "I'm an idiot," he said in apparent amusement. He threw open the driver's-side door and walked past her. The trunk clicked open from behind.

No, no, no.

Aiden flung open her door. In his hands he held a roll of duct tape and a knife. Her gut seized, and she began screaming. "Don't put me back there. Help! Somebody help me!"

Aiden peeled off a strip of tape and then sliced it with the knife. "Knew I should have done this to start with," he grumbled, leaning toward her with the improvised gag.

She rocked her head violently back and forth, but Aiden still managed to slap the tape across her mouth. *I can't breathe.* Her lungs burned. Would she die from asphyxiation before they made it to wherever he was taking her? She inhaled as much oxygen as she could through her nose, but it didn't feel like nearly enough.

"The front gate guard isn't there now, but they might have a camera recording my coming and goings," Aiden mused aloud, as calmly as though deliberating a move in a chess game.

Then he picked her up and carried her once again. She wiggled, trying to leverage her bound body to either butt him in the head or twist from his grasp, but Aiden was too strong, too determined, for her struggles to even slow down his inevitable next move.

Aiden stuffed her in the trunk and slammed the lid shut. Cold darkness enveloped her, and even though no one could possibly hear, Beth whimpered, her screams smothered and trapped under the tape. The closed confines felt like being entombed in a metal casket. *Stop. Get ahold of yourself. There must be something you can do.* She quit screaming but her loud, labored breathing roared between her ears— and still she couldn't seem to suck in enough air. Giving in to hysteria and hyperventilating would not help her live to see the morning.

Beth controlled her breathing to a slow, dia-phragmatic pace. Her eyes adjusted to the dark-ness and in the taillights' pinprick glow she discovered a large metal toolbox in the right corner. She kicked it with her bound feet and it toppled over, its contents spilling out—rough lengths of cord, several knives, black gloves and rolls of duct tape.

Aiden had come prepared.

Beth held her breath, wondering if Aiden had heard the toolbox fall. But he drove on, still humming along with the loud radio music, as though he hadn't a care in the world. And why not? He thought he was smart enough to get away with murder.

But despite all his cool, deadly arrangements, Aiden hadn't factored in her desperate will to fight for her life, or her ability to devise a plan of her own. As far as he was concerned, she didn't have the brains or the brawn to fend off an attack.

She'd just have to prove him wrong.

With the toolbox knocked on its side, Beth discovered another tiny source of light that shone in the trunk's dark interior—a small handle with a dim glow. She stared at it, wondering what it opened.

Understanding thundered in her brain. A release handle! For at least the past decade, all vehicles made in the United States were required to provide an interior trunk release mechanism. She wanted to cry with relief.

Beth rolled over to it and tried to maneuver her body into a position where her bound hands could pull the handle. Her first priority was escape. She'd work on her bindings next. But no matter how she twisted, her hands couldn't quite grasp it. At last she gave up, panting through her nose, exhausted with the effort. Beads of sweat dribbled down her forehead, stinging her eyes, yet she couldn't swipe them away.

The sedan came to an unexpected halt and Beth stilled, dread churning in her stomach. Seconds later the vehicle rolled onward, and she realized Aiden had stopped at the stop sign at the bottom of Falling Rock. What kind of psychopathic killer obeyed traffic signs in the dead of night when no one was around?

She tried to keep her bearings and figure out where they were going. If—no, *when*—she got out of this damn trunk, she needed to know where she was. How awful it would be to have a chance of escape only to run around in circles and get caught by Aiden again.

If Aiden stayed straight on this road, they'd soon be in town. If so, it would be her best opportunity to kick the trunk lid and hope that the noise would attract attention. But who would hear her? No one would be on the streets at this hour. There had to be another way. She'd read newspaper stories of people escaping from trunks. What had they done?

An image flashed through her mind, a television reel of a kidnapped child who'd kicked the taillights out of his abductor's vehicle and then stuck his hand through the resulting hole, alerting other motorists that he was trapped inside. She'd do the same, but she'd have to wisely choose her timing. Aiden would surely hear the noise of the taillights shattering. The most opportune moment to make her move would be at the first traffic light in town. With luck, there would be a few late-night travelers for the holidays and someone would see her desperate signal for help.

But instead of going through town, Aiden took a sudden left. Her small ray of hope immediately extinguished. They were on County Road 18, heading away from Lavender Mountain's town area. What ungodly, remote place did Aiden have in mind for her murder?

Okay, scratch the whole kick-out-the-taillights plan. No way would there be a stray vehicle on this lonely mountain road. If she was going to get out of this alive, it was all on her.

Beth searched in the semidarkness until the palm of her right hand came into contact with sharp, cold metal. Now was the time to try to cut her hands free of their bindings. More likely she'd slice her wrists open in the awkward, blind attempt and then proceed to bleed out. But anything was preferable to whatever Aiden had in mind for her.

Cautiously, Beth gripped the knife's handle and began to saw at the rope binding. The top of the blade pricked into her wrist, but she gritted her teeth and readjusted her aim. It was painstaking work and she repeatedly stabbed at her own flesh in the process, but what choice did she have?

To help keep her mind off the pain and the imminent danger of her predicament, she continued to try and map their location. Did he have their burned-down cabin in mind? They were headed in that general direction, but going there didn't make sense. There was no reason to choose it as a murder scene. Perhaps Aiden would arbitrarily stop on this lonesome road whenever he decided the time was right.

The rope bindings began to ease under the wet slickness of her wrists. The sedan suddenly swerved, and she lost her balance. Searing pain sliced through her skin as she fell against the knife blade. Beth moaned and caught her breath, trying again to slip out of the restraints. Her time was short. Aiden had turned onto Witches' Hollow Road and that only led to one place.

She knew exactly where they were going. This was a dead-end lane that ended at an old abandoned gravel pit. Estimated at over sixty feet deep, this time of year the pit would be filled with icy water from melted snow. Her brother's intention couldn't be any clearer. The only question now was whether he intended to kill her before throwing her into the icy pit.

Branches raked against the vehicle in an eerie grinding that set her teeth on edge. The road was narrowing, and the sedan jostled as it ran over potholes.

The binding at last gave loose and Beth freed

her hands. Quickly, she ripped the duct tape from her mouth, barely registering the tear of flesh on her face. She gulped in a lungful of fresh air, grateful for the small mercy.

The sedan hit a deep pothole. Her entire body lifted and then dropped. At least this time her arms were free, and she could stabilize herself from rolling all over the trunk. The vehicle slowed as the terrain worsened. Aiden couldn't continue much farther down this path without a four-wheel-drive truck. She was almost out of time. Beth hurriedly cut off the rope binding her ankles. It was now or never.

She located the trunk release lever and popped it. A sweet click, and the top of the trunk flung open, blasting her with the night's frigid air. Beth grabbed one of the knives and lunged forward. The sedan came to an abrupt halt.

"What the hell?" Aiden thundered, opening up the driver's-side door.

Beth scrambled out of the truck and began to run. Her ankles and feet were numb from being bound, but she stumbled forward as fast as she could.

"Stop running," Aiden shouted.

Hell, no. Why should she make her murder more convenient for him?

A shot rang out, exploding into the night. She

kept running, waiting for the shock of the bullet as it rammed into her, but nothing happened. She dared not glance behind to see what was happening. Aiden must have fired that warning shot straight up in the air. Beth cut away from the road, slipping into the cluster of trees and dense foliage. Aiden was hot on her tail as she rushed forward, branches and vines cutting into her face, hair and body. This must be what it was like to be a deer or rabbit fleeing from a hunter—only she was the one out of her element here in the bleak, alien woods. Her left foot caught under a root and she fell. Her ankle twisted and burned beneath her. The knife fell from her hands. Beth hunkered down, gathering her body into a tight ball under a knot of woody bramble that cut through her clothes and into her flesh. Her fingers searched for the knife, but all she felt was snow melting into her bare hands.

Dead leaves and twigs crunched all around where she lay on the wet ground. Closer and closer he came. Beth closed her eyes, awaiting the inevitable. All she had left was to try and land a good kick or punch once he discovered her hiding place.

And he would find her.

She knew the moment Aiden spotted her. All sound ceased. A whoosh of air and then a bruising grip ground into her right forearm. Aiden placed a knee against her back. She tasted snow and leaves.

"There you are. Did you really think you could get away from me? Damn, killing you is more trouble than I thought it would be."

"Aiden. Please. You don't want to do this."

"Got no choice now. We've come this far."

The distinctive sound of duct tape unraveling rent the air. Seconds later, her shredded and bleeding wrists were taped. Tears gathered in her eyes. She'd worked so hard to be free and now she was right back where she started.

"I won't tell anyone what happened tonight."

He snorted, not even bothering to point out how ridiculous she must sound. With a grunt, he yanked her to her feet.

"At least you wouldn't get the death penalty if you stop now," she persisted, hoping to reach him by some wild chance. Deep down, she believed some shred of humanity still existed beneath his charming, light-hearted manner. "Quit and maybe you'd end up with only a few years in prison for kidnapping."

Past his shoulder, a cut of light strobed through the trees. It lasted only seconds, then vanished. The dark seemed darker and more absolute from its absence. Had she lost it? Had desperation and fear conjured an illusion?

Aiden whipped his head around and surveyed the woods, then shrugged. "Must have been lightning."

Lightning was an unusual phenomenon in winter, though. She didn't have time to dwell on it as Aiden began dragging her back toward the road.

"Don't give me any more trouble," he warned. "Accept your fate and you won't have to suffer. It will all be over quick. But if you do fight me, I'll knock you out cold. Your choice."

Some choice. Stay conscious and face Aiden while he killed her in order to have one last shot at begging for her life and praying for a miracle, or take being knocked out and spared the final horror. Beth decided to fight until the end.

"Someone saw us, Aiden. Those were headlights flashing through the woods. They'll report it. A car with a popped trunk on a dark road? They're probably calling it in right now. Let me go and you can get away."

Aiden ignored her. He crammed her into the front seat and then settled beside her. "I want you where I can see you. How the hell did you manage to get free?"

She didn't answer and rapidly scanned the center console and dashboard for either a cell phone or a makeshift weapon. Only a couple of empty beer cans lay scattered on the floorboard.

"I don't want a blood trail everywhere," Aiden continued. "I'm hoping they never find your body. That way, there's less risk anything will ever be traced back to me."

He cranked the car and the sedan lurched forward. They proceeded slowly, but with the deteriorated condition of the road the sedan scraped ground a couple of times. Beth's gaze switched from Aiden's profile to the wild landscape. In minutes, the car headlights shone on a faded metal sign that read Lavender Mountain Pit & Quarry. Just beyond the sign was a ramshackle wooden building that had once served as the company's modest headquarters. She'd visited the place many times over the years as a teenager. Local legend maintained that the structure was haunted, and it had become a Halloween attraction for older teens looking for spooky thrills. Beth never imagined the creepy place would be the sight of her own violent death.

The car shuddered to a stop and she cast him a quick glance. *Wait until he pulls you from the car, then make your move.* That would be her best shot at making contact.

Unexpectedly, Aiden reached across her and pushed the passenger door open. "Get out," he ordered. She froze, unsure if now was her moment to strike.

"I said get out." Aiden gave her a violent push and she tumbled out. Aiden immediately followed suit. "Turn around," he commanded.

Slowly, she obeyed. He stood before her, illuminated in the car's elliptical beams. He had a gun raised and aimed directly at her. Beth's heart beat painfully in her chest. With his head, Aiden motioned her forward. Behind him, the black abyss of the pit awaited.

But they weren't alone. Someone was watching. She heard a twig break, as if snapped by a foot. She felt them staring, watching in the darkness like a wild beast. Beth crept forward at a snail's pace. Past Aiden's shoulder, a figure emerged out of the woods. Moonlight glowed on his ginger hair. Recognition slammed into her.

What the hell was Dorsey Lambert doing out here? Were he and Aiden working together?

Aiden studied her startled face and then whipped his head around. But Lambert had already disappeared into the shadows.

He chuckled. "You really think that old trick's going to work on me?"

Chapter Seventeen

The phone rang, jostling Sammy from an uneasy sleep. The alarm clock by his bed blinked neon-green numbers—2:46 a.m. Nothing good ever happened at this time of day. Could it be Beth? He picked up his cell phone from the nightstand and frowned at the unfamiliar number. Not Beth then. His racing heart quieted several beats. But an Atlanta area code was on display. Perhaps there was some news about Dorsey Lambert. Quickly, he swiped the screen and spoke. "Officer Armstrong."

"Sammy?" A woman's hesitant voice sounded. "I'm so sorry to bother you at this horrible hour but I'm afraid."

"Who is this?"

"Cynthia Wynngate, Beth's stepmother."

Sammy stood, pulling on his uniform pants he'd flung at the foot of the bed only a couple of hours ago. "What's wrong? Is Beth hurt?"

"I—I'm not sure."

"Explain yourself."

"We, um, had a bit of a falling-out earlier today. I don't know if she told you?"

"She did," he growled impatiently. "Go on."

"So I asked Aiden to go over and try and help smooth things over between us like he always does."

His heart slammed in his ribs before he remembered Beth was spending the night at Lilah's. Sammy pulled on socks and slipped into his uniform shoes. "Your point?"

"I—I think Aiden might be planning to hurt Beth."

Sammy stilled, hands frozen over the shoelaces he'd been tying. All his niggling doubts and suspicions about his old friend rushed up and merged into a knot of dread. "What makes you say that?" he asked past the lump in his throat.

"It wasn't so much what he said, it's how he said it. His practice hasn't been going so well and when I called him this afternoon, I asked how his firm was doing. He admitted it was in dire straits but that he had a plan to fix everything." Cynthia paused. "He sounded strange… I—I can't explain it exactly. I pressed him what that meant, and Aiden claimed he'd be coming into a large sum of money in the next few weeks. I asked if a big lawsuit settlement was due and he laughed, saying he had a major score to settle with someone."

Sammy cradled the cell phone between his shoulder and right ear as he slipped into his uniform shirt. He wished Cynthia would hurry with her story, but suspected that the more he interrupted and pressed her, the longer it would take.

"Anyway, I asked when he'd leave to see Beth today and he said he had a few supplies to pick up first before leaving the city. Then— and this is what makes me nervous—Aiden said tonight was the night his plan would be set in motion and that people like Beth, born with silver spoons in their mouths, didn't deserve to have such easy lives when people like him had to struggle."

Sammy scowled. What a strange woman Cynthia was to report her son to an officer of the law on the basis of so little. "And from that conversation you suspect your own son... of what, exactly?"

Her voice chilled a notch. "I'm just saying maybe someone should check on Beth. I awoke from a disturbing dream over an hour ago and I've tried to call both of them but get no answer. I even tried the landline at Falling Rock."

Why hadn't Beth answered her phone? Probably only because she saw Cynthia's name on the screen and didn't want to talk to her, he suspected.

"I'll check it out," he told Cynthia, abruptly ending their call. Immediately, he punched Beth's number on speed dial. It rang four times and went to voice mail. "Call me," he said roughly, not expecting to really hear from her. Beth was either asleep or had her phone ringer turned off. To be safe, Sammy called Harlan to make sure all was well.

"Sampson here," Harlan grumbled into the phone. "Sammy?"

"I'm calling to make sure Beth's safe and sound. I got a call from her stepmother warning she might be in danger from her stepbrother."

Harlan muttered an expletive. "She's not here. She left hours ago, insisting that she wanted to stay in her own home. Sorry, I should have called you. Do we need to—"

Alarm coursed through him. "I'm going over now to check it out. I'll call you later."

Sammy buckled his belt and headed to the den where he grabbed the Jeep keys off the fireplace mantel. Recrimination rose and battered his conscience. He should have asked Beth if he could spend the night with her. He couldn't rest now until he'd either seen Beth or heard her voice.

Chills skittered down the back of his neck as

he raced out the door and into his Jeep. Sammy zipped down his neighborhood street and then sped through town. At the entrance of the Falling Rock subdivision, the unattended gate opened automatically, and he shook his head as he drove through. Months ago, their home-owners' association had cut back on manning it with a security guard on duty at nights, citing the difficulty of finding and funding personnel. In his opinion, the gatehouse was now merely a pretentious show of wealth and security that held no real teeth.

Most of the homes were tastefully lit with a Christmas tree placed in an open window and outside strings of white or pale lights draped across porch and roof lines. A few homes had mangers or decorated yard trees that glowed from a single white spotlight. Driving through the elegant neighborhood felt like slipping into a fairyland. Could anything really bad happen here?

Oh, hell yes. Sammy recalled the human traf-ficking ring they'd uncovered a year ago. A wealthy Atlanta couple had used one of these mansions as a holding pen for kidnapped young women. While there, the victims were physi-cally and emotionally broken down and even-tually sold as sex slaves. His partner, Charlotte, had been the one to crack that case.

He turned the corner to Beth's street and gave a brief, involuntary smile at the corner house, which sported over a dozen inflatable holiday cartoon characters, including a twenty-foot-tall Grinch. The home was lit with a mismatch of bright colors on every available surface. Some might unkindly call it "tacky," but he secretly loved it.

Sammy's amusement was short-lived as he pulled into Beth's driveway. His knot of anxiety wouldn't unravel until he saw she was unharmed. Leaving his truck running, he ran to the front porch and stopped, his heart sinking.

The front door wasn't completely shut; it gaped open an ominous inch. Sammy withdrew the revolver on his belt clip and stepped to the side of the door before pushing it open all the way with his foot.

There was no sound or movement from beyond. Slowly, he eased into Beth's home, gun drawn. He stole past the unlit dining room, down a hallway and into the den where a lamp burned near the sofa. At first glance, all appeared in order. Sammy peered closer at the sofa where Beth might have recently sat. Semidry droplets of a dark liquid spotted the floor and couch cushions. Had Beth had an accident of some sort? Or had something worse befallen her? His own blood ran cold at the thought.

Sammy raced upstairs to check out the bedrooms. All were empty and there were no signs of a struggle. Beth's bed was unmade, as though she'd been in it for a time before being awakened. Where had she gone in the middle of the night? He hurried back downstairs and opened the garage door. Her rental car was parked inside. Sammy strode over to it and placed his hand on the hood. It was cold and unused. He opened the door and took a look. Nothing unusual there.

Sammy returned inside, his concern mounting. He called Beth's phone number again and heard it ring nearby. He found it plugged into a charger on the kitchen counter, next to her purse. His shoes squeaked, grinding against some small object. His eyes followed the trail to several large fragments of broken glass. Behind the kitchen island were larger pieces of broken glass, perhaps a vase.

He called her name, then Aiden's. Nothing. Just the sound of his own voice in the empty home.

Beth had not left her home willingly. Not without her purse and phone. He called Charlotte on speed dial. She answered almost at once, although her voice was drowsy with sleep. Sammy found himself suddenly unable to speak past the massive pressure weighing on his chest.

"Sammy? What's up?" Charlotte's voice sharpened. "What's wrong?"

"It's Beth," he said roughly. "She's missing. Foul play suspected."

A muttered curse and then "Where are you? I'm coming over."

He gave her the address. "Call Harlan, too," he added. "We need a manhunt with all available officers."

"Should I put out an APB on Dorsey Lambert?"

"Yes. And also on Aiden Wynngate."

"The man in the videotape. Beth's stepbrother, right?" Charlotte asked.

"Right. I'll explain everything later."

He hung up the phone and swiped a hand through his hair. Who had taken Beth—Lambert or her stepbrother? Were they working in tandem? It would make sense. Aiden's firm represented persons charged with a crime. As the tape had shown, Aiden had plenty of opportunity to make connections with the criminal underworld.

Think. Where would Aiden or Lambert have taken Beth? Trouble was, there were dozens of remote roads in these mountains. All suitable for murder and burying the victim in a shallow grave that might or might not be discovered by hunters one day. His heart pinched, imagining Beth at this moment, scared out of her mind, believing she was about to die.

Or she might already be dead.

Sammy drew a long breath and shook his head. He couldn't go there, couldn't entertain the thought of Beth not being in this world. They'd find her. There had to be a clue here somewhere. He scanned the kitchen and his eyes rested on a stack of papers on the table. That was as good a place as any to start his search. He glanced at the typewritten words and blinked.

Last will and testament of Elizabeth Jane Wynngate.

Frost flowed through his veins and his heart froze. Abruptly, he rifled through the papers and found what he was looking for. Aiden Wynngate was listed as the primary beneficiary, with his mother, Cynthia, also inheriting a significant percentage. If Aiden had an accomplice, it was Cynthia, not Dorsey Lambert. But why would Cynthia have called him if she was in on it? Maybe she wanted to make sure the finger pointed at her son and not at her?

Unless this was an elaborate red herring planted by Lambert. Sammy immediately struck that idea as not being credible. Everything pointed to Aiden. His strange behavior, association with criminals and one terrific financial need. Greed was always a slam-bang murder motive.

Where would Aiden take her? He knew all these backroads. Even with a full-blown manhunt it would take hours to check every narrow dirt road that crisscrossed the mountains. His cell phone rang, interrupting his racing thoughts. He glanced down at the screen before answering. It was Charlotte.

"We've got a tip," she said without preamble. "An anonymous caller at the station claimed a woman had been abducted and taken to the old Lavender Mountain quarry."

The old abandoned pit. Of course. He should have thought of that straightaway. "On my way," he said tersely, tucking his phone in his back pocket, then fishing the Jeep keys from his pocket as he ran to the door.

He could be there in ten minutes, twice as fast as any officer in town. But would that be quick enough? It had to be.

Sammy sped out of Falling Rock and raced on the snowy rocks with reckless abandon. *I'm coming, Beth. Hold on, sweetheart.*

He hadn't been to the quarry in years and he almost missed the turnoff. Sammy slammed on his brakes and took the turn like a NAS-CAR driver on the final lap of a race. The Jeep swerved to the far left, almost plunging into a ditch before he jerked the steering wheel to the right and returned to the road's center. Headlights illuminated recent tire tracks in the snow.

Almost there, Beth.

The truck bounced and rattled on the rough road. All at once, he came upon an unmoving sedan and had to slam his brakes to keep from plowing into its rear fender. Sammy swerved to avoid the collision and the car beams spotlighted two persons standing near the edge of the deep pit—Aiden, eyes wide with shock and bleeding from a cut at his temple, and Beth, looking equally as shocked, her brown hair whipping in the wind.

Sammy retrieved his gun and flung open his truck door, using it as a shield. From the side of the door, he pointed his gun at Aiden. "Hands up, Wynngate."

Aiden pulled a gun from his jacket and fired a round. Pain exploded in Sammy's left shin and his leg gave out beneath him.

"Run, Beth!" he screamed, rolling under the Jeep bed for protection. But he wasn't fast enough. Another bullet slammed into the front of his left shoulder, dangerously close to his heart. He lay on the ground, exposed and vulnerable. The next shot would take him out for good. Had Beth run? Was she safe? A black film seemed to form over his vision, and the world grew fuzzy and unfocused.

A shrill scream pierced through the ringing in his ears. *Beth.* He opened his mouth to urge her again to run, but the words would not come. He struggled to his feet. If it was the last thing he did, he had to shoot his old friend. Had to protect Beth at any cost. Her life was all that mattered. Tamping down the pain, he picked up his gun in his right hand and focused.

Aiden had walked closer to him and only stood a few feet from where he lay, gun raised for the lethal shot. Beth lunged at Aiden's back and he fell. A shot exploded, and Sammy felt a bullet whizzing by his ear, narrowly missing his face. Beth was still in danger. Why wouldn't she run while she had the chance? Aiden's gun lay on the snow-covered ground between them. Sammy began crawling toward it. Aiden also crept forward to retrieve his weapon. Beth lay sprawled on the ground, stunned from the impact of hurling her body at Aiden.

He was going to die. They both were.

From his right, a figure sprang from the dilapidated quarry headquarters. Was he hallucinating? Just as Aiden's fingers grasped the weapon's handle, the man kicked the gun away. Beth scrambled to pick it up.

"Sammy! How bad are you hurt?" she cried.

Dorsey Lambert's eyes locked with his. What the hell was the man doing here? Were the two in league after all? No, that made no sense. Lambert had saved his life.

In the confusion, Aiden jumped to his feet and began running. Dorsey took off his jacket and pressed it against Sammy's wound. The pain was excruciating but necessary. He could feel the warm blood soaking his shirt and jacket.

"Backup on the way?" Dorsey asked. "I called the cops earlier."

"Yes."

Beth dropped to her knees beside him. "Sammy!"

"He's going to be okay," Dorsey said. "That bastard was trying to frame me for murder. I knew I had to keep an eye on him."

Sammy hoped Lambert was right in his pronouncement that this shot wasn't fatal. Even now, sirens wailed in the distance. But his head swam, and strength oozed from his body with every drop of blood lost. And still Beth wasn't out of danger. "Aiden might return," he warned them. "We…" His words began to slur. "Not safe yet. Still in danger."

Chapter Eighteen

Still in danger.

Beth cast a quick glance over her shoulder in time to see Aiden hightailing it to the woods. She knew what she had to do. She'd already witnessed her stepbrother's persistence. He'd come back to finish them off if he had the chance.

"I'll stay with him until the ambulance arrives," Dorsey said with a nod at Sammy. "You go on. Know how to use that gun?"

"Yes." But she hesitated, staring down at Dorsey's hands pressed over Sammy's wound. Blood had soaked through Sammy's jacket and covered Lambert's fingers. Sammy's eyes were closed shut and his face was pale as the snow. Fear clinched her gut. She didn't want to lose him. Not when her heart had begun to love.

"Go!" Lambert shouted, thrusting a flashlight into her free hand. "There's nothing you can do here."

Beth rose to her feet and ran, gripping the gun's handle in her right hand. She knew how to use it but hoped she didn't have to. All she needed was to keep Aiden in sight and make him quit running. The cops could arrest him then and take care of the rest.

She shone the flashlight on Aiden's footprints in the snow. He couldn't escape. Not after all the hell he'd put her and Sammy through. She'd brought this trouble into Sammy's life. Aiden was *her* stepbrother and he'd been after *her* money. Only fair that she be the one to bring him down in the end.

She entered the woods, and the thick tree canopies blocked most of the full moon's light. If Dorsey hadn't had the good sense to bring a flashlight, she wouldn't have had a chance at tracking Aiden. Surprisingly, a narrow trail ran through the terrain. Probably forged by deer hunters, she surmised. Aiden had somehow found the trail. Had he scouted this area ahead of her abduction? Had he devised contingencies in the event he was forced to flee? What if he'd deliberately drawn her into the cover of the woods?

Beth flicked off the flashlight. What she'd imagined an advantage might prove her undoing, since the elliptical beam spotlighted her every move. Her heartbeat went into overdrive and she felt the roaring of blood in her temples. Despite the cold, a sweat broke out all over her body. She strained her ears, listening for the slightest whisper of Aiden's breathing, of an unexplained twig snapping.

But there was only the persistent, haunting howl of the wind rattling through the treetops. An owl hooted, and she bit back a scream. Seemed she'd gone from hunter to hunted. *I'm the one armed with a gun. Aiden's the one who should be frightened, not me.* Yet her mind didn't buy the argument. He was close, she could feel it. She had to know where he was. Waiting in the darkness for him to pounce was the worst torture. Beth snapped on the flashlight and circled around.

No Aiden in sight.

Her legs went weak with relief and she leaned against the rough bark of a pine tree. Chasing Aiden was a fool's errand. She'd go back to Sammy and wait for the cops to mount a search. They were the experts. She straightened and turned for retreat.

Straight ahead, the flashlight illuminated a large obstacle that hadn't been there seconds before. *Aiden.* The light trembled in her hands and she almost dropped it. He'd been so quiet in his approach. So lethal.

He grinned. "Hello, Beth."

How could he be so calm—so confident? He'd greeted her as though he'd just stepped into her home for a chat, as though they weren't standing in the woods after he'd attempted to kill both her and Sammy. The grip on the gun at her side tightened. Did he have a weapon, as well? One he'd hidden here earlier?

He stepped forward and she took a step back, raising the gun. "Stay where you are."

A smile ghosted across his lips. "You wouldn't hurt me."

"Don't be so sure."

He didn't take another step, but he didn't retreat, either. "Why, Aiden?" she said gruffly, past the lump in her throat. "Have you hated me all these years?"

"Not always. At first, you were merely an inconvenience. But once your father died, you were in my way."

His words were more chilling than the December night. *In the way. An inconvenience.* How could she never have seen past his easygoing facade? She wanted to believe there was some good left in him. A modicum of decency.

Aiden stretched out a hand. "Give me back my gun."

She shook her head, trying to wake up from the surrealistic nightmare of the last hour. "Why should I? So you can shoot me?"

"I won't hurt you. I just want to escape. I can't go to prison. It would kill me."

The sirens sounded louder, and he uneasily glanced behind his shoulder. But would they get here in time? She had to keep Aiden focused on her, not the approaching cops.

"Did Cynthia murder my dad?" she asked, hoping the question disarmed him and returned his focus to her.

He faced her again and chuckled. "Good ole Mom. She's inventive, you've got to give her that. Put her LPN training to good use."

"What did she do to Dad?" Beth fought back her tears, her horror. "How did she kill him?"

"*Kill*'s a strong word. Come on. Your dad was old and had a weak heart. He'd have died soon anyway. Mom only helped him along a little."

"How did she do it?" she insisted, her voice tight and hard. "I never heard even a whisper of suspicion on the cause of death."

"After his heart attack, Mom finished him off with an air embolism. Killed by thin air." Again he chuckled. "All it takes is a well-administered syringe of oxygen." He held up a hand and pointed his thumb and index finger like a pistol. "Poke that tiny needle in an inconspicuous place and voilà—an easy solution." He jabbed his index finger above his kneecap and made a tiny, swishing sound. *Whoosh.* "Like I said, she picked up a thing or two at her old job."

The callous description of her father's murder almost shattered the little bit of her composure that remained. Her knees jellied, and the gun wobbled in her hand. Beth struggled to understand why this had happened to her family. "But why? He loved you. Both of you. He took you in and shared everything he had."

Aiden shrugged. "Stop making him out to be a damn saint. He was a dirty judge, remember? You always were in your own little world, painting and drawing. But to answer your question, he got suspicious of Mom having a boyfriend. She denied it, of course, but Mom was afraid that since he was onto her, he'd hire a private detective and find the truth."

Aiden took a step forward, but this time Beth didn't step away. Anger steadied her hand and gave her strength. The sirens kicked up a notch, their ghastly wail drawing closer. The longer honk of a fire engine blasted, as well as the high-low pitch of an ambulance alarm. *Please let them get here in time for Sammy.* He'd have been so much better off if he'd never gotten involved with her. But on the heels of that disturbing realization, Beth realized she could never regret a moment of their time together.

The memory of every second—every kiss and every touch—seemed incredibly precious.

"One last question."

He quirked a brow and stilled.

"Does Cynthia know about…about your plans tonight? Are you two working together?"

Aiden flashed a grin, his teeth gleaming as white as the snow in the darkness. "Are you kidding me? Her methods are more subtle. More untraceable. Mom doesn't have the stomach for the nitty-gritty work."

If she couldn't appeal to Aiden's humanity, perhaps she could reason with his avarice. "You know she gets a large hunk of my money when I die, right? You don't get it all."

"Do you think I'm stupid?" His mouth tightened, and his chin lifted an inch. "I'm an attorney, for Christ's sake. I can read a damn legal document. I know exactly how much she'd receive. But she won't live to enjoy it."

Matricide. Cynthia was a lot of things, but she adored her son. Aiden was her golden child that she protected and defended. Maybe that was the problem. She'd raised him to believe that he deserved anything he wanted and to claim it at any cost.

Aiden was upon her, his breath smelling of bourbon. "Give me the gun. Now. You'll never see me again."

"I don't believe you."

"It's true. I've got a car and a driver waiting for me down the road." He pulled a small leather binder from the inside pocket of his jacket. "Got a passport and a plane ticket, too."

"Where do you think you can run?"

"Like I'd tell you?" He shook his head. "All I'll say is it's warm and their cops turn a blind eye to extradition requests. But I need my gun. I can't outrun the cops without a weapon. There's going to be a standoff."

Alarm chimed through Beth. He'd need more than a weapon. He'd need a human shield. He'd need...*her.*

The woods were suddenly alive with blue and red cop lights strobing through the icy trees and dense underbrush, sirens shrieking in the frigid air—the moment of reckoning was upon them. Aiden's arm began to rise, and she made a move of her own. Her left arm hoisted the heavy steel flashlight in an arc, catching the right side of his face in a crushing thump of bone.

Aiden screamed and staggered backward, holding his head in his hands.

Beth dodged around him, navigating clumsily through the copse of trees. *Head back to the main road.* She didn't need the flashlight now; the glare from first responder vehicles cast a spotlight on the clearing ahead. Aiden clomped behind her, as fast and furious as a bull and gaining on her with every second. Her wet slippers were useless for gaining traction.

She reached the clearing. Several police cars snaked across the narrow road and a couple of them left the road and bumped across the field. Their headlights stung her eyes and she blinked, trying to orient herself in the temporary blindness.

Oomph. A solid mass of weight slammed into her back. An arm encircled her throat, pushing her neck back in a choking hold. She could hardly breathe.

Aiden had gotten just what he wanted. He'd take her down with him if needed. What else did he have to lose?

"Give me the gun," he growled in her ear.

The gun. Thank heavens she hadn't dropped it. He might be faster and stronger, but she wasn't defenseless. Cold metal practically burned into her numbed hand and fingers. Could she do it? Really shoot somebody? Hell, yes. He'd left her no choice. As best she could in the awkward hold, Beth aimed the gun backward and pulled the trigger.

The explosion rang in her ears. The hold loosened, and Aiden screamed in agony. She gulped in a lungful of fresh air. Cops seemed to shout at her from every direction, but she was too wired to make out the words, only the frantic urgency of their voices. *Run.* Aiden wasn't through with her yet. Just as her legs obeyed her brain's command, Aiden lunged at her, knocking her to the ground.

The gun fell out of her hand and she grabbed it. Aiden loomed above her, his dark eyes aglow with desperation and madness and anger mixed with fear. He raised an arm, his hand gripped in a fist. She tried to wiggle out of his grasp but his knee lodged firmly in her gut and his left arm anchored her upper torso. The snow was wet and freezing, seeping through her bathrobe and pajamas. In two seconds Aiden would deliver a knockout punch, take her weapon and make his wild dash to freedom while dragging her along as a hostage. He'd kill her at the first opportunity when she was no longer useful to him.

Beth lifted the gun, not sure if she'd even get off a shot before Aiden's fist shattered her face. With numbed, stiff fingers, she pulled the trigger and fired. The reverberation of the gun tingled in her palm and the blast deafened all sound. All sensation seemed frozen in the frigid night. A chiaroscuro of black, white and grays punctuated with slashes of red.

There was Aiden's widened eyes and slackened jaw;

…the crimson patch blooming on his chest;

…the black nighttide lit by red sirens;

…the white snow falling swiftly and silently—a silent witness to murder.

Oh, God. She'd killed him.

Aiden's body toppled backward several inches and then fell forward. She watched his descent in horror. There wasn't time to move away. Dead weight crushed her chest. Beth screamed until her throat burned raw. Pandemonium erupted as cops and rescue workers arrived, their voices calling out sharp commands and urgent warnings. A volley of camera flashes strobed the area from officers recording the crime scene.

It was all a jumbled mess echoing round and round in her brain. Strong arms rolled Aiden's heavy, slack body away. "Is he…?"

She couldn't form the word, but the man nodded. He had a kind, grandfatherly face that was worn and wrinkled. He awkwardly patted her arm. "Sammy?" she asked.

"They've already taken him to the hospital. Are you hurt?"

Beth eased up to a seated position and blinked at the swarm of people standing above. Two men placed Aiden's lifeless body on a stretcher. She averted her eyes, not wanting to witness the shell of a man she'd believed had cared about her all these years.

"I'm okay but I want to go to the hospital. I need to be with Sammy."

She struggled to her feet, surprised to find her limbs weak and her vision blurry. Two people rushed forward and supported her from either side.

"Need a stretcher?" one of them asked.

She stiffened her spine and cinched the wet, dirty bathrobe closer against her waist. All she needed was Sammy. She had to be with him, to touch him and see his eyes open again.

Not ten yards away, an ambulance awaited, its back door open and the interior lit. She glimpsed two stretchers and lifesaving equipment on shelves. But there was also another vehicle—the side of it emblazoned with the County Coroner seal. Several workers loaded a stretcher with Aiden's body wrapped in a tarp.

The cops waved an EMT crew over and she was encircled. Safe and protected. But a tight knot of anxiety cramped her stomach.

Please, God, let Sammy live.

Chapter Nineteen

Beth laid her head beside Sammy's chest on the hospital bed where he rested. Despite the uncomfortable chair, she was afraid that if she fell asleep it would be days before she awakened. The weariness went bone-deep. She'd showered in Sammy's private room and Lilah had brought her dry clothes to change into. Her friend, mother hen that she was, had also insisted that she eat a bowl of soup. Now, warmed and sated, her body wanted sleep. She fought the drowsiness, wanting to be the first thing Sammy saw when he awakened.

The doctors had assured her that the surgery to remove the bullet and staunch the internal bleeding had been a success. A couple of nights in the hospital for observation and Sammy could go home.

Home. Beth realized that she thought of Lavender Mountain as her home now. Boston seemed far, far away. Her heart was here in

Appalachia—with Sammy. The hospital door opened and Lilah poked her head in, eyebrows raised in question. Beth shook her head no, shuffled to her feet and entered the hallway where Harlan and Lilah stood guard.

"He's still sleeping, which is a good thing. Sammy needs lots of rest." She cut Harlan a stern glance. "He's in no shape to be giving statements or making reports tonight. Probably not tomorrow, either."

Harlan nodded. "Of course. Besides, I spoke with him just before he went under the knife and I know everything I need to for the time being. I also spoke with Charlotte before she was admitted here."

"What happened to her?" Beth hadn't even known Sammy's partner had been on the scene. Dread weighed on her chest. Had something awful happened to the pregnant cop?

"She's fine," Lilah assured her with a quick squeeze of the hand. "Just delivered a nine-and-a-half-pound baby boy. James is beside himself. It's their first baby."

Lilah and Harlan exchanged a tender, knowing smile as Beth sighed with relief. At least something good had come out of this night. "Y'all should go on home," she urged them. "Sammy's out of danger and I'm fine."

Lilah leaned into Harlan's side, patting her

round stomach. "I'm not going to argue with you. I'm beat. Come by whenever you're ready. The spare room's yours."

Harlan extended a hand toward her. "You'll always be welcome in our home."

She shook his hand and his unexpected kindness had her blinking back tears. No wonder Lilah was so in love with this man. He often appeared taciturn and aloof on the outside, but underneath, Harlan was a solid, stand-up kind of guy. Lilah had chosen well.

Beth tiptoed back into the room and resumed her seat by Sammy's bed. Some color had returned to his face and the chalk-white paleness was gone. His breathing was smooth, deep and regular.

She huddled under a blanket. After all the hours outside in the winter cold, it seemed her body just couldn't get warm enough. Her lids were heavy, and she gave in to the pleasant lethargy.

Something tugged on her hand and she startled awake. Beth gazed at the unfamiliar, sterile room in confusion for a moment until her eyes focused on Sammy. He smiled at her, his brown eyes warm and gentle. "They told me you were okay," he said. "But nothing beats having you right here in front of me where I can see for myself."

"Ditto," she said past the lump in her throat. "You gave us all a scare."

"Nothing compared to what I saw when I found you with Aiden."

She nodded slowly. "You know he—he's dead now."

"Harlan filled me in on everything. Don't you dare waste a moment of grief for his sorry ass. You did what you had to do."

"I know, but…"

Sammy held out his arms, and she leaned forward, laying her head on his chest and allowing him to comfort her. For the first time since she'd arrived at the hospital, tears slid down her face. But they were good tears this time, healing tears. Sammy's fingers caressed her scalp and then his fingers stroked her hair. Beth sighed and felt peace settle over her at last.

Long, long minutes later, she pulled away. "Forget about me. You're the one who's been shot. How bad does it hurt?"

"I told you I'm fine," he said gruffly.

"If something had happened to you…" Beth squeezed his hand.

He narrowed his eyes. "Sure everything's all right with you? You must be exhausted. And devastated."

"Aiden's not the worst of it. It's what he said about Cynthia that I can't get out of my head."

"Cynthia?"

"Oh, that's right. Harlan didn't get a chance to fill you in on everything. Aiden claimed that she killed my father by injecting him with oxygen. Apparently, an air embolism did him in."

"Damn it. None of us even suspected there was foul play, Beth. Given his age and history of heart trouble—"

"Of course you couldn't have known." Beth stood and began pacing. "I don't know what to believe anymore. If what Aiden said is true, I want Cynthia to pay for what she did to Dad."

Sammy frowned. "Don't expect a confession from her. And I seriously doubt that there's any evidence after all this time."

What about justice for her father? Had her stepmother gotten away with murder? Beth hugged her arms into her chest. "Do you think Cynthia killed him?" she asked Sammy.

"We may never know for sure, but I'm inclined to think the answer is *yes*."

"Me, too." She recalled the grim amusement on Aiden's face as he described how his mother had caused the fatal heart attack. "Harlan told me she called you and rang the alarm about Aiden. Why do you think she warned you I might be in danger?"

"Could have been one of two things. Either

she wanted Aiden caught in the act and arrested, leaving her with your inheritance—"

"Or she truly cares about her son and wanted him to get caught before he killed me and possibly ended up on death row," she said slowly. "I'm guessing it's the first option."

"And she might have tipped us off to cover her bases in case an investigation implicated Aiden. That way, she could claim she acted in your best interests over her son's, even throw doubt on any stories he would tell about her possible involvement in your father's demise."

"I bet she hates me now," Beth muttered. "Not that I particularly care about her opinion. Unless she decides to come after me for shooting Aiden."

"You'll never have to see her again, whether or not she's ever convicted of murder. I won't let her hurt you," Sammy promised, his face grim and his eyes flashing in fury. "Soon as I'm able, I intend to have a little chat with her. I guarantee you by the time I'm finished, she'll never want to step within miles of anywhere you might be. If she knows what's good for her, and I suspect a person like her always has their best interests at heart, Cynthia Wynngate will never again step foot in the State of Georgia."

Beth believed him. "There's only one thing left that troubles me."

"What's that?"

"Dorsey Lambert."

"No need to worry on his account. The man saved both our lives tonight."

"That's what I mean. I feel like I owe him."

"You don't owe him a thing. But if it makes you feel better, we can write a letter to the parole board recommending he be released from parole."

"I want to do more than that. After all, my Dad did take his money and placed an undue hardship on his family." She stopped pacing and nodded her head, decision made. "I'm going to provide him a reward. Enough money so that he can start over in a new life."

"That's incredibly generous. Probably more than he deserves. He and his family did stalk you, remember? They also broke into your home and tried to extort money from you."

She cocked her head to the side and regarded him with a smile. "But they weren't killers. And Dorsey saved your life. For that, he deserves a fresh start."

Beth resumed pacing, her heart growing lighter as she thought of the future. There were so many things she wanted to do, so many wrongs to right. As the daughter of a judge, no matter how much her father had erred later in life, her sense of justice ran deep. And she had her dad to thank for it. For many, many years he'd been honest and fair. Whatever had corrupted him later, she'd grown up with his strong role model of integrity.

It was how she'd choose to honor and remember her father.

Her right foot knocked against something on the floor and she glanced down to find what she'd stumbled upon. A black duffel bag was positioned at the end of the hospital bed.

"Harlan brought it over," he explained. "I asked him to bring that and—"

"What's this?" She lifted the square canvas that had been leaning against the bag. She held it up to the fluorescent overhead light and chuckled with surprise. The edges were charred, and soot blackened a good portion of the bottom, but she recognized it as one of the paintings she'd been working on at the cabin.

"I can't believe you kept this."

"Are you kidding me? I risked life and limb to get them."

She laughed. "Crazy man. It wasn't worth it."

"Sure it was. It's beautiful. And you painted it."

She couldn't tear her eyes from the ruined painting. She could redo it, or even try and repair the damaged parts. But Beth decided she wanted them to remain. They were a reminder of the day Sammy had run out of the burning cabin with a handful of her artwork.

The day she'd fallen in love.

"Come here," Sammy demanded gruffly, patting the hospital bed.

Beth propped the painting on the metal night-stand and climbed into bed beside him. She ran a hand through his hair, and he planted a kiss on her forehead. "So you think I'm a crazy man?" he teased, his chest rumbling with laughter. "I'll admit, I'm crazy in love with you."

It was hard to believe her heart could go from the depths of despair from only a few hours earlier, to feeling as though it would burst with joy. His admission left her speechless. She knew how deeply his parents' divorce had affected his willingness to make commitments.

"I'm not asking you to stay here," he said quickly. "I know you have a life in Boston. But we could see each other long-distance. Plenty of couples—"

She kissed him, long and hard. At last she pulled away. "I don't want a long-distance relationship. I want to stay right here in Lavender Mountain."

"But won't you miss the excitement of Boston?" His brows drew together in consternation. "What about all your artsy friends and visiting museums? We have nothing of the kind to offer here."

Did he want her to stay or not? Was he still afraid of love and commitment? "I see unparalleled beauty in the Appalachian Mountains that no museum painting can ever replicate," she said quietly.

Sammy appeared unconvinced. "What about all your friends? Your art classes?"

"I can teach anywhere, including Lavender Mountain. And as far as friends and family, all I ever want, or need, is one person who loves, supports and believes in me." She jabbed a finger playfully in his chest. "And that person is you. I love you so much."

"I love you more. But are you sure? Really sure?" Hope flickered in his dark brown eyes, but she also read a worrisome, nagging doubt.

"One hundred percent positive," she assured him. Then she pressed her mouth against his, expressing all her love in the kiss. She was where she was supposed to be, now and forever. Sammy held her in his arms, and long after he'd finally fallen asleep, Beth lay beside him in utter peace and joy as she watched the snow fall on Lavender Mountain.

* * * * *

Get 4 FREE REWARDS!

We'll send you 2 FREE Books <u>plus</u> 2 FREE Mystery Gifts.

FREE
Value Over
$20

Both the **Romance** and **Suspense** collections feature compelling novels written by many of today's bestselling authors.